The Jacob portfolio

For the family:
Andy and Jenny, Peter and Gill,
who try to keep me on track.

The
Jacob portfolio

Ambition, love and God

Derek Wood

Inter-Varsity Press

INTER-VARSITY PRESS
38 De Montfort Street, Leicester LE1 7GP, England

First published 1990

British Library Cataloguing in Publication Data
Wood, Derek, 1934–
The Jacob portfolio
1. Christian Life
I. Title
248.4

ISBN 0–85110–853–9

Typeset in Great Britain by Selectmove Ltd.
Printed and bound in Great Britain by
Courier International Ltd, Tiptree, Essex

*Inter-Varsity Press is the book-publishing division of the
Universities and Colleges Christian Fellowship
(formerly the Inter-Varsity Fellowship), a student
movement linking Christian Unions in universities and
colleges throughout the United Kingdom and the Republic
of Ireland, and a member movement of the International
Fellowship of Evangelical Students. For information
about local and national activities write to UCCF,
38 De Montfort Street, Leicester LE1 7GP.*

Contents

From the author

People sometimes ask me whether Canwell Park, SW31, is a real place. It all depends on what you mean by 'real'. The District Line goes no further than Wimbledon, and Canwell Park may be on no map of the London area, but the characters who live there are real enough to be quite a handful.

I mean, it's quite easy to plan to write a book and to map out a story, but the people in the story have an unsettling knack of taking over and doing and saying things which the author hasn't planned. It's sometimes difficult to keep up with them and to make them behave as required.

It is frustrating not to be able to let them develop their characters in depth, but there's very little room for manoeuvre in 160 pages, so some major changes happen rather too suddenly for comfort. But then, the writer of Genesis condensed the whole of Jacob's life into eleven chapters, so who am I to complain?

My thanks again to Marie Palmer for typing the manuscript from my hasty scrawl (who says all authors have word processors these days?) and, among others, to Jim Saker for helpful advice. And thanks, too, to the inhabitants of Canwell Park who have allowed me access to their thoughts as well as their actions. I find it a great privilege.

Derek Wood

1

'What have we let ourselves in for?'

'**I**t's a quarter past.'

Sallie Peterson looked across the deep-pile hearthrug to the sofa. Two legs, clad in severe grey trousers, appeared to be propping up a copy of the *Financial Times*.

The imitation coal fire hissed gently but nothing else stirred.

'I said, it's a quarter past,' said Sallie more loudly. 'If we don't leave now, we'll be late.'

The *Financial Times* sank slowly like a drawbridge and revealed the handsome features of Nigel, bronzed from their recent skiing holiday in the Alps; dark, almost black hair above a square-cut face with a very determined chin.

'Must we?'

'We jolly well must,' said Sallie, rising from her armchair.

'Well, you'd better do a quick change and wear a longer skirt,' said Nigel. 'You realize where we're going, don't you?'

'Do you really think so?' Sallie was dubious. 'They can't be all that narrow-minded.'

'Well, I wouldn't take any chances. We don't want to embarrass anybody, do we? His wife is probably a dreadful scarecrow with a bun and baggy trousers. If you go dressed like that he won't be able to keep his mind on the subject.'

'You kept your mind on the *Financial Times*,' said Sallie, sticking out her lower lip petulantly.

'Well, we're both agreed about what really matters in the world, aren't we? But don't let's start an argument, Sallie, or we'll never get there.'

Sallie ran up the oak staircase and returned a few minutes later wearing a white blouse with a severe collar and a grey suit with a knee-length skirt.

'Will I do, darling?'

'Perfect,' said Nigel, kissing her on the nose. The heavy front door clicked shut. 'His or hers?'

'His' was a large, cream BMW, owned by finance brokers Crieff-Farbsteen in the City of London, and driven by Nigel, their rising star, twenty-eight years old and eager to get to the top.

'Hers' was a bright red TR7 in which Sallie sped round the neighbourhood of Canwell Gardens, the exclusive executive town house estate on which they lived.

'Oh, I think you'd better drive, dear,' said Sallie. 'It's a rather chauvinist world down there, I expect.'

A luxuriance of honey-coloured hair contrasted dramatically with the black leather coat that Sallie had put on over her suit. Nigel thought that the street lamps showed her to great advantage. What would these people make of them? And in any case were they doing the right thing? Their life together had been as good as it could possibly be, not perfect but built on shared values and romantic love. Their house was all that they could have hoped. The mortgage was astronomical but their joint income coped with it. Sallie was twenty-five and already well on the way up the ladder in her firm of accountants, Drew, Drew & Drew.

They had agreed that the basis of their relationship was a shared determination to succeed. Opportunities were there to be taken. People were sometimes in the way, but often they made rungs to ascend the ladder by. Not that Nigel or Sallie were heartless or cruel people. They were a normal, red-blooded young couple with clear-sighted aims and goals and they had agreed to combine their talents into a formidable partnership. But this evening they were the very reverse of confident.

'We promised'

The BMW rolled to a standstill behind the queue of vehicles at the end of Fairview Avenue, waiting to negotiate the War Memorial roundabout. Round the corner, into High Road and they would be there. It had been a two-and-a-half-minute drive. Some would have walked. Yet even now they could escape. On their right, the warm, inviting bow window of the snuggery of 'The Auld Alliance', Canwell Park's best pub. A quick left turn instead of right and they could be in Town in half an hour and going to a show.

Their eyes met.

'You know we've got to do it, Nigel. We promised Mummy.'

'Well, OK. I know you're right. The Old Man was pretty definite as well. They know they've got us where they want us with this moral blackmail.'

The 'moral blackmail' was a gift of £10,000 each from Nigel's and Sallie's parents as part of the down payment on their house. They not unreasonably expected something in return.

'We promised, Nige.'

Nigel forced the wheel to the right, round the War Memorial, into High Road and almost immediately right again into the Vicarage drive. It was exactly half past seven. Never had Nigel had to call on more will-power than he expended in pushing the doorbell.

Light streamed out, framing the figure of an attractive, dark-haired woman in her mid thirties, who was wearing a skirt shorter than Sallie's. Perhaps they had a maid?

'Hullo! I'm Diana, Timothy's wife. We're expecting you. Do come in. Isn't the traffic *awful*!. . .Tim, dear, they're *here*!'

Diana ran down the passage to find her husband.

'A dreadful scarecrow, with a bun and baggy trousers,' whispered Sallie with an ill-concealed giggle.

'H'm, yes. Could be worse,' admitted Nigel. 'I'm beginning to be glad I came.'

There was no time for Sallie to aim her handbag at Nigel's head before Timothy appeared and was beaming at them and shaking them by the hand. Timothy was more what they had expected of a vicar, rather older than his wife, hair receding a little, dressed in a comfortable, baggy sweater and trousers that had moulded themselves to their owner.

'Coffee?' Diana was back. 'Decaff? Black?' To Sallie and Nigel's surprise Diana stayed with them instead of delivering the coffee and retiring discreetly to her kitchen.

'We might have known'

The formalities had to be met and forms filled in. Name: Nigel Daberon Fitzpaine Rogers, Grande Corniche, Farcroft Crescent, Canwell Gardens, SW31; bachelor, date of birth. . .

Name: Sallie Claire Peterson, same address. . . Sallie thought that Diana's eyelids flickered at this point but Timothy went on writing without comment. Nigel maintained afterwards that he had not been looking at Diana's eyes and so could not have seen them flicker. The formalities were completed and Sallie was preparing to leave when the blow fell.

'We can't demand this of course,' Timothy was saying, 'but we make two requests of our couples and we expect them to make these commitments. We expect you to attend a course of marriage preparation classes, one a fortnight, and to attend church once every Sunday, morning or evening, between now and your wedding day.'

'But as for "living in sin" as you put it, we're living in sin too.'

Diana stretched out a hand and her husband took it affectionately. Nigel and Sallie suspected a trap at this point so neither said anything.

'The Christian view,' said Timothy, 'is that everybody, without exception, is sinful, because "sin" means falling short of God's perfection. We can't help living in a state of sin. To apply the phrase to sexual matters only is a confusion. Sexual sins are not the only ones, in fact not necessarily the worst, in spite of what the tabloid newspapers seem to want us to believe.'

'Am I to understand,' said Nigel, 'that, in order to be married at your church, you are expecting us to switch our whole view of the human race from being generally well-meaning, natural, intelligent beings to a morbid, medieval pack of grovelling, sin-sodden morons?'

Sallie looked admiringly at Nigel. He could be quite eloquent sometimes.

Timothy laughed. 'No, I'm not,' he said. 'The whole point of the Christian faith lies in forgiveness. Yes, we are sinners, but the sin can be cancelled. That's what Jesus Christ came to earth for. But look, we can't go into all this now. That's the reason why we ask people to attend the course and come to services, so that we can put the point of view clearly and mop up a lot of misconceptions. Will you do it?'

'It doesn't seem as if we have much choice,' said Nigel after a pause. 'Would you marry us if we refused?'

'There are registry offices,' said Timothy. 'If you're not at all interested in the Christian way of looking at life and marriage, the registry office is the proper

15

place for the wedding. But I sincerely believe that the Christian view of marriage is one that will give you a much better chance of staying together and living in mutual respect and love.'

'Well, then, I suppose we *haven't* much choice,' said Nigel, looking at Sallie, who remained silent.

'It's not as dreadful as all that, you know,' said Diana. 'I think you'll enjoy it. We've got three other couples so far. It should be great fun. It's just like being sent on a course by your employers, to qualify you to do your work better. Marriage is more important than work so it's more important to prepare for it properly.'

As Sallie and Nigel said their goodbyes and the door shut out the light once more, Nigel looked up at the black bulk of St Barnabas' church with its great tower and spire reaching beyond the glare of the streetlamps. He shuddered.

'We're going to have to go in there, you and I,' he said.

'What have we let ourselves in for?' said Sallie. 'Still, we're in it together, aren't we?'

Twenty-five seconds later the BMW stopped again, in the car-park of 'The Auld Alliance'.

■ If you're not a church-goer, what is your idea of churches and church people?
■ If you are, how do you think non-church-goers think of you and your church?

2

Jacob: career step one

Jacob rested his forehead on his hands to shut out the glare of the westering sun. His handsome features were bronzed but not burnt, his black hair hidden beneath the linen *keffiyeh*, his determined chin accentuated by a profusion of beard.

The hot wind flung a sudden acrid stream of smoke into his face and he turned away, spluttering. He got up and, approaching the fire from the windward side, stirred the contents of the great pot hung above the flames.

Jacob asked himself for the hundredth time what he was doing stirring a stewpot while his elder brother Esau was out with the goatherd hunting. Goatherd? They left the goats for Jacob to look after while they spent the day in the wild. It was not that he wanted to be out there with them. He wasn't jealous in that sense. He felt much happier around the encampment where they lived. But he was bored by doing nothing at home, jealous of his brother, persecuted by his father Isaac and spoilt by the over-fond attentions of his mother, Rebekah. He was in an impossible situation with no obvious way out.

It was all due to an accident of birth. Jacob sometimes wondered whether his birth had not in fact been an accident altogether. Esau was his elder brother. Esau therefore would inherit the lion's share of their father's possessions and all the spiritual pre-eminence that came with a father's blessing: a very powerful and mysterious inheritance. The elder brother. That was the irony of it. Esau was only a few minutes older than Jacob. They were twins. If twins were ever born simultaneously they could hardly have been closer. Jacob was born actually grasping the heel of his brother, as if to signal to the world that he was not satisfied with second place but would hang on until he had got what he wanted.

Names meant a great deal in those days and the name 'Jacob' was variously interpreted by family and acquaintances as 'he who grasps the heel' (the politer version) and 'swindler and deceiver' (more often behind Jacob's back). The circumstances of his birth, the reaction of his family and the long years of relative inactivity had settled Jacob's character into that of a morose and patient spider, ever spinning his scheming webs and waiting for his prey to entangle itself there. He saw the world as his enemy, its inhabitants as his rivals and its God as his judge, or perhaps his benefactor, if he could be persuaded to take Jacob's side for once.

Stirring the pot

Then there was the prophecy. Rebekah had often told him of the prophecy. It wasn't clear by that time whether she had heard God speaking to her or whether someone, perhaps the midwife, had spoken. Isaac refused to believe a word of it. Then, he would. Esau was the apple of his eye.

The words of the prophecy were: 'The older will serve the younger.'

There wasn't much sign of the prophecy coming true, thought Jacob as he stirred the stew again, rather too vigorously. The steam hissed on the outside of the pot. 'Pot-stirrer for a turnip-headed brother who just happens to be a few minutes older than I am. What a destiny!'

There was a hoarse shout and Jacob looked up. Why, here he came, this red-faced lout of a brother of his, dragging the carcase of some innocent animal, slaughtered for sport. Then he would eat it (Jacob was an ardent vegetarian) and give some to Isaac, and Isaac would say how good it was to have real meat again after putting up with Jacob's bean stew, pea stew, bean and pea stew, pea and bean stew; was there no end to it?

Esau flung down the carcase in the shade of the tent awning and stretched himself out beside it.

'Great day, Jacob, great day.' His hoarse voice was even louder than usual. Perspiration made tracks down the rugged dust-stained face in red and brown stripes.

Jacob shuddered and turned away.

'That smells good,' said Esau, propping himself on an elbow and sinking back again as if the effort had been too great.

'It's not for you, brother dear,' said Jacob. 'There's no carrion in it. It's bean and vegetable stew. It wouldn't suit a carnivore like you.'

'Give me some.'

'I beg your pardon?'

'You heard what I said, give me some. Now.'

Jacob was used to this kind of treatment but there was an edge so uncouth and almost bestial in the way that his brother spoke that something seemed to snap in Jacob's mind. He turned suddenly to the pot and was on the point of heaving it up and dashing the whole seething mass into Esau's face when he stopped and looked slantwise at his brother.

'Brother?'

'Ahuh?'

'How hungry are you?'

'Don't ask stupid questions, boy. I'm famished.'

'What will you give me in exchange for a good meal?'

'What have I got to give you except this?' Esau patted the carcase affectionately and wiped the blood on the floor. 'You don't want a share of this, do you?'

Jacob paused. Was Esau really crass enough to fall for his suggestion? Well, he couldn't lose anything by trying.

'You have a birthright, Esau.'

'A birthright? Oh, *that*! I thought you were after something real. You can have that with pleasure.'

'Are you serious?'

20

'Of course I'm serious. What's the use of a birthright if you're about to die of starvation?'

'Swear an oath, then.'

'Oh really, Jacob, you are tiresome. You have to make a melodrama out of everything. If I don't get a meal soon I shan't have the strength to swear even.'

So Esau swore his oath and Jacob gave him an unusually generous helping of bean and vegetable stew. Jacob struggled hard to keep the jubilation from showing on his face. 'The fool, the unutterable fool,' he thought as he watched his brother scalding his silly mouth as he gulped the stew.

But Esau was not quite the fool that he seemed. What difference did a few words make? The birthright was not a written document. Clay tablets were not part of the nomad's equipment. He was still the elder; no oath could change the facts. And he was still his father's favourite. As long as the supply of meat kept coming he was pretty safe there. Jacob really was rather gullible. A schemer, a swindler, but he didn't seem to understand the value of brute force.

'More stew, brother, more stew!' Esau was feeling better.

The registry office

Nigel Rogers was feeling worse. They had stayed longer than they'd meant to at 'The Auld Alliance' last night and the marmalade was tasting odd this morning.

Sallie looked pale and was not talking much.

'Of course I agree with you that our living together is right. There's no question about that,' said Nigel, 'but the point is that these people *think* it's wrong and that means that we haven't much in common with them. They really are living in the Dark Ages. I think we should scrap the whole idea of church and go for the registry office. Monteith was right there. If we can't go along with them we shouldn't pretend.'

Sallie pursed her lips and said nothing.

'If it was just going through the motions on the wedding day I could cope,' Nigel pushed his plate away, 'but it's all this preparation course and going to services that worries me. The other people on that course will all be pure as the driven snow. They'll faint if sex is mentioned.'

'Bun and baggy trousers,' murmured Sallie.

'Oh, all right, I'm exaggerating again, but they go out of their way to make us feel guilty. They'll have a job to make me feel guilty.'

Sallie remained silent.

'What's the matter, Sallie, are they getting to you? Are *you* feeling guilty?'

'No,' said Sallie, 'I'm not, but we can't get married at the registry office. Mummy. . .'

'Mummy! I knew it would be Mummy. Our life is like a music-hall joke. It's the mother-in-law who rules from darkest Suffolk. We don't *have* to obey Mummy, you know.'

'No, but she did give us ten grand.'

'Ten, yes, but that's not much really.'

'It's as much as your dad gave us.'

'OK, but it was a gift, remember, not a loan, repayable if we refuse to have a church wedding.'

'Mummy hasn't been too well recently.'

'You won't win me over with sob stuff.'

'Not sob stuff, Nigel. She might die. I am her only child, remember. She has much more than ten grand.'

'Do you mean she'd cut you out of her will just because her Gothic fantasies can't be acted out at our wedding?'

'She might,' admitted Sallie. 'She's been getting very tied up with animal rights and things like that. It would be just like her to have a fit of pique, change her will on behalf of the dogs' home and then pop off suddenly before she'd had time to reconsider.'

'Fit of peke,' muttered Nigel. 'I must work on that one.'

'What?'

'Pique: peke.'

Sallie got up suddenly. 'If half a million means nothing more to you than making silly jokes then we're getting off course. I've got to get to work.'

Nigel dropped the remains of his breakfast into the disposal unit and stacked the dishes thoughtfully in the dishwasher. Half a million. She'd never mentioned that much. Registry offices were very impersonal places, after all. . .

And so the great decision was made.

- The story of Jacob's birth and the episode of the 'sale' of Esau's birthright are from Genesis chapter 25 verses 21–34.
- Has this chapter been fair to the original?
- How alike are Nigel and Jacob?

3
Chalk and cheese

Sunday morning. Twenty-five minutes past ten. St Barnabas' church, Canwell Park. Nigel and Sallie present themselves at the arched doorway, feeling like two lambs about to be slaughtered.

Inside there is a murmur of voices, an organ playing softly and an indefinable smell – a mixture of dust, polish and dampness.

'Good *morn*ing! How *nice* to see you!' A man in a grey sweater was shaking them by the hand. Nigel glanced down at his pinstripe suit and wondered whether he had overdone it. Sallie was risking nothing but had dressed again in her severe blouse and grey suit.

Into their hands were thrust three books, one of them very thick, and they were ushered into two vacant places on a pew which had a piece of carpet on it. Out of the corner of her eye Sallie noticed someone else who had just come in kneeling down before taking her seat, so she motioned Nigel to do the same. There were hard stuffed cushions to kneel on, each with outlandish embroidery, doves holding olive branches, lambs holding flags and dragons with spears sticking into them.

Nigel buried his head obediently in his hands and counted slowly to fifteen. He glanced nervously at the lady opposite. She was now seated so he risked looking up.

At that point the organ music seemed to change gear and, without any other sign, everyone stood up. Nigel leapt to his feet and dropped all his books on the floor. Sallie glared at him. This was dreadful. And now came two male figures, apparently dressed in female night attire, walking solemnly down the centre gangway, smiling benignly. One of them was Timothy. His smile broadened as he passed Sallie and Nigel, but Nigel was on his knees, picking up his books, and Sallie was too embarrassed to smile back.

Timothy announced a welcome and looked straight at Nigel and Sallie again and then told them they were to sing a hymn. After a slight problem as to which book the hymn was to be found in they tried to keep up with the tune and mouth the words, which, however, were quite meaningless to them. The strange thing was that the people around them seemed to find the singing enormously satisfying. They sang lustily, some raising their hands in a kind of ecstasy, others closing their eyes and swaying gently:

'Crown him the Lord of peace,
Whose power a sceptre sways
From pole to pole. . .'

What had got into these people?

'The service begins on page 119 in your prayer books.' A hundred and nineteen? Why not page one? The page numbers were very small and the paper very thin, so it was difficult to locate the correct page, but everyone else seemed quite at home.

Just as Sallie was beginning to get tired of standing, a Bible reading was announced and everyone suddenly sat down, leaving the hapless pair standing for a further two seconds, which felt like two minutes. Ah. So that was it. When the Bible was read you sat down.

Another Bible reading was announced.

Everyone leapt to their feet, leaving Nigel and Sallie sitting, with their usual two-second pause. After the reading they all said something incomprehensible about 'Christ our Lord' and watched Timothy climb the steps into his rostrum. He closed his eyes, said a prayer, and everybody sat down again.

This was the sermon. At least they could relax their vigilance for a few minutes. It turned out to be twenty-one minutes, by which time Nigel and Sallie had completely lost track of what Timothy was saying. It was about a character from thousands of years ago called Jacob, who, according to Timothy, had completely the wrong attitude to life. He had all the privileges in the world, apparently, and was in direct line with Abraham as one of the patriarchs of the Chosen Race, and yet he descended to double-dealing and swindling his brother. And his father. And his uncle. It was a sordid business but Timothy's voice was pleasing. The atmosphere became quite comfortable. . .

'A people of power'

Nigel was jerked back to consciousness by the sudden appearance of half a dozen rather scruffy youngish people, bearing guitars, a violin, an accordion and tambourines. Reinforced by an amplifier the volume of their sound was surprising, but the tune was simple and vigorous.

They were all on their feet again, singing with enormous gusto, clapping hands, stamping feet and waving at the roof. 'A people of power' and 'Build your church, Lord' seemed to be the subject of the song. Obviously it went down well, as they had three encores, and even Nigel and Sallie began to get the general drift of the tune.

After more similar songs and a solemn recital of what everyone apparently believed and which Nigel and Sallie listened to politely, there were more prayers, then they stood up again and Timothy said, 'Let us offer one another a sign of peace.'

If the service had been full of surprises already, none could equal this. People were acting like children suddenly let out of school. A hubbub of voices broke out. They were shaking each other by the hand. Some were embracing. The words, 'The peace of the Lord be with you' seemed to be the thing to say, over and over again. Nigel found himself pumped by the arm by a beaming middle-aged man, who said, 'We haven't met before. I'm Bob.'

Sallie found herself almost lifted off her feet from behind by a huge lady who clutched her to her ample bosom and said, 'Peace, luvvy, peace. What's yer name, ducks? I'm Connie.'

After what seemed like ten minutes, but was in reality four or five, peace really was restored and the service went on.

'Why do they say hello in the middle and not at the beginning?' hissed Nigel as Sallie attempted to get her breath back. But before she could attempt an answer, Gordon Barber appeared at her elbow with a collecting plate in his hand.

Gordon Barber, late thirties, rather bald, was the church treasurer. Sallie did not know that, but she did know Gordon Barber. In fact he worked for the same firm of accountants, Drew, Drew & Drew. They were not on terms of close friendship, but she knew that he was rather religious. That didn't seem to matter just now. It was such a relief to see a familiar face. Even if there was an offering plate below it. While she was exchanging a few brief words with Gordon, Nigel whipped out his wallet and placed the smallest available amount (a ten-pound note) in the plate and passed it thankfully on.

Next there was a kind of parade when the money collected was taken to the front and ceremoniously placed on the table laid there with a white cloth. There was also a silver tankard there and a plate. The full horror of the situation dawned first on Sallie.

'It's communion,' she whispered.

'It's *what*?'

'Communion. Bread and wine. What shall we do?'

'We can't get out now.'

But Bob Renshaw, on Nigel's left, had seen what was happening and explained to him that they were quite welcome to sit in their seats if they wanted to, or they could if they wished, go and stand in front of Timothy and be prayed for. Perhaps later, decided Nigel, when they felt a little stronger.

This was obviously the most solemn part of the service because a door opened in the side of the church and in rushed dozens of children, all clutching papers and coloured streamers which they had been making. They were not noisy children, but the atmosphere was definitely different when they came in.

So Nigel and Sallie watched in wonderment as long files of people solemnly moved forward to stand in a semi-circle round the table at the front to eat a little bread and drink a little wine. When each semi-circle had finished, its members linked hands for a few moments and smiled at each other. For some totally ridiculous reason Sallie found that she had tears in her eyes and had to look away. Nigel was staring dumbly at the hymn book. So this was what happened in churches, all over England, all over the world. There were millions of people, ordinary sane people, who went through this kind of activity every week. It was a completely new world. Nigel prided himself on being unshockable, able to stand firm in every crisis. But this was extraordinary. Would they ever get used to it? Horror of horrors, perhaps they would. Perhaps one day they too would know which page they were on and what 'ineffably' meant and be able to smile at each other like that.

'Bob will be on his own'

The service was over at last and Sallie made for the door and freedom. But her way was blocked by the huge bulk of Connie Bassett. Connie had originated in London's East End and had spent most of her life entertaining in 'the halls' as she put it, but she had recently found a totally new kind of life (as chronicled in *The Simon Peter file*) and had been dramatically baptized in the swimming baths before a large crowd of well-wishers. The event had made the local newspaper, *The Canwell Clarion*, with the predictable heading: 'CONNIE MAKES A SPLASH'.

She had become a vigorous member of the church, rounding up quantities of fellow inhabitants of 'The Haven', the old people's home in Station Road.

Here she was, blocking Sallie's way, beaming at her and thrusting a cup of steaming coffee into her hand.

'Connie,' she said again. 'Connie Bassett.'

Then Gordon Barber was smiling broadly at her, introducing her to his wife, Margaret, and his daughter Shelley. Shelley was eight and was clearly impressed by what she saw of Sallie.

'Do you watch "Top of the Pops"?' asked Shelley earnestly.

'Not very often,' replied Sallie.

'"Metal Virgin Caterpillar" has gone to Number One this week,' said Shelley. 'They've got a great hit called "Grandfather Ice-bottle". Do you know it?'

Sallie kept a straight face with great difficulty while Margaret finally managed to replace her daughter.

'Shelley, how often do I have to tell you?'

Margaret obviously had to tell Shelley so often that what she had to tell her was left unsaid.

Sallie explained to Margaret and Gordon that she and Nigel were intending to marry at St Barnabas'. Nigel was telling Bob Renshaw the same story and so it was that all five of them gathered round the coffee table.

'You must come round and have a meal with us,' said Gordon. 'Don't say, "Yes, perhaps we will one day", because one day will never come. Have you got your diaries? Fix it now, even if it's six weeks away, and we'll know it's arranged.'

Nigel produced the inevitable Filofax from his inside pocket.

Margaret looked at Sallie.

'Oh, it's all right. Nigel keeps all the fixtures. I'll make a note of it later.'

A date was fixed, while Bob carefully studied his coffee. Margaret saw what was happening.

'Bob,' she said, 'you'll come as well, won't you? The house is big enough for more than four, you know.'

And so it was arranged. Margaret, Gordon and Shelley were walking up Fairview Avenue as the BMW swept past and cheerful waves were exchanged.

'Nice pair,' said Gordon. 'Pretty well-heeled by the look of it.'

'Yes,' said Margaret distantly, 'but Bob will be on his own.'

'On his *own*? What do you mean? There'll be five of us.'

'Six,' said Shelley.

'Five, Miss Barber. You will be in bed.'

'I'm always in bed,' muttered Shelley, looking for a stone to kick and not finding one.

31

'What I mean is,' said Margaret firmly, 'there'll be two couples, and Bob will be left out. We must invite someone else.'

'It's not a dance; he won't need a partner,' protested Gordon.

But Margaret had made up her mind.

'I'll 'phone Gina,' she said. 'She'll round off the evening very well.'

So Gina Holwell wrote 'Supper with G and M' in her diary and wondered what was afoot.

- Can you remember going to an unfamiliar church?
- What did it feel like?
- If you are a regular church-goer, can you sympathize with Nigel and Sallie?
- How does your church compare with St Barnabas' in welcoming newcomers?

4

Jacob: career step two

The dust settled, the shouting grew faint and peace returned to the encampment. Jacob heaved a deep sigh as his brother Esau set out on one more of his hunting expeditions. Where he got the energy from Jacob could not imagine. He turned to go indoors, rubbing his eyes to free them from the fine particles of dust which seemed to penetrate the very pores of his body.

One day he supposed he would go blind too. His father was blind. Not because he was an old man yet but because of the dust. His mother, Rebekah, could see very clearly, but she always wore her veil in public. Perhaps that helped. There she was now, standing at the edge of the cooking area.

She was looking straight at him and beckoning him.

'Jacob, my son. It's good news at last.'

'We haven't had any news at all for three weeks, mother, not since the camel train went by.'

'Listen, Jacob. Your father thinks he's going to die.'

'Oh, so that's good news! I knew you didn't get on all that well, but that's rather a black joke.'

'Be quiet for a moment and *listen* if you can. I said he *thinks* he's going to die. Of course he isn't really. Apart from his eyesight the old fool is as fit as a fiddle, but the point is that he has decided to give the Blessing of the Firstborn.'

'The Blessing of the Firstborn? That means he really does think he's dying. Are you sure he's all right?'

'Quite sure.'

'Well, Esau will become the head of the family, the Patriarch, and my gaining the birthright will count for nothing. He'll have God on his side then. I can't take on an oaf of a brother and Elohim at the same time. Oh, I knew something like this had to happen. Why was I born to such trouble? Why was I born at all? And you said it was good news! Good news for Esau. What kind of good news is that for me?'

'Jacob, will you stop clucking like an old hen and pay attention? Your father has sent Esau off to catch some supper for him. When he comes back there'll be a great boil-up and a feast and the culmination of the evening will be the Blessing of the Firstborn. . .'

'That's what I say. What's the good news if Esau gets the Blessing?'

'Jacob gets the Blessing.'

'Jacob gets the. . . Mother, you're mad!'

'Your father is blind.'

'Yes, but he's not a fool even if you did call him that. Anyway, how do you know all this?'

'I was listening. You don't think they'd have asked my opinion, do you? What you should do is listen to my opinion now. You've always prided yourself in your imitation of Esau's voice. You've often had us in stitches round the camp-fire. Now's your chance to put it to good use.'

'But he won't trust his ears. He's a suspicious old bird. And anyway, how can I go hunting and catch one of these creatures and kill it – *kill* it, if you please! I think I should throw up. Even if I could hunt, which I can't. It's all impossible.'

'What are those?' Rebekah's voice was studied and patient.

'Goats, mother.'

'Goats. We choose a goat from the flock. You look the other way. I kill it and make a savoury stew of it. He won't know what kind of meat it is as long as it has the right herbs with it, and I know the recipe. As for the disguise, you can leave that to me too. Remember, he's expecting Esau. The mind plays strange tricks. The very outrageousness of the idea makes it all the more likely to succeed.'

'If he finds out, he'll kill me.'

'He's too weak. And he *is* blind.'

'Well, he'll curse me instead of blessing.'

'I'll take care of the curse, Jacob. You just go and choose a goat and leave all the rest to me, there's a good lad.'

For once Jacob did not protest when his mother used that phrase that had patronized him ever since he could remember. He undid the latch and entered the goats' enclosure.

'Like the smell of a field'

Isaac settled himself on his bed. He was looking forward to Esau's return. A couple of hours, perhaps, and then he would have his hunter back home and he would sit up and eat once more the game stew. . .and then, the Blessing of the Firstborn. He rehearsed the words of the Blessing again in his mind. Just as his father had blessed him, so he would bless his son. God's promises were being fulfilled in his family.

A shadow clouded the warm glow of his vision.

'Who's there? Who is it?' Isaac struggled to sit up.

'Esau, my father.'

'What? Esau? Already? It can't be! You've only been gone three or four hours. How have you got back so quickly?'

'The Lord your God brought the herd straight to me. All I had to do was to choose a couple of beasts and they fell at my feet.'

'The Lord be praised!' said Isaac, but with less conviction than Jacob would have liked. 'Have you cooked it already?'

'Can't you smell it, Father? Your sense of smell has gone the same way as your eyesight.'

Isaac was troubled. Something was wrong. There was an oddness about Esau's voice. It sounded clipped and subdued.

'Your voice sounds strange, Esau.'

'I've been out for four hours in the heat. Swallowing dust. I think your hearing is failing as well. You'd better have something to eat quickly.'

Isaac had never realized how similar Esau's voice was to Jacob's. He had always thought of them as very different. Now, suddenly, he was hearing their similarity. It would be hard for Jacob. Poor Jacob. Never the favourite, but he stayed at home and worked hard. It was a pity in a way that Jacob would get nothing out of this business.

'Come and embrace me, my son,' said Isaac suddenly.

This was the crunch for Jacob. If Isaac felt the difference between them (Esau was covered in hair like a wild goat) this would be the end. Jacob bent low over his father's bed, making sure that Esau's best hunting cloak would fall near the old man's face. It was a tense moment. Isaac's hand wandered over his son's shoulders and arms. It encountered only animal skins. The stench of them was as disgusting to Jacob as it was a delight to his father. The old man sank back on his pillow with a smile on his face.

'I thought it was Jacob's voice. Wasn't that strange? But the coat and the hands are those of my son Esau. Call the servants to be my witnesses! Help me to sit up now. Ah, the smell of my son is like the smell of a field that the Lord has blessed.'

Then Isaac ate a symbolic morsel of meat, drank a sip of wine and placed his hands on Jacob's bowed head, and spoke the words of the Blessing of the Firstborn, the words that can never be retracted nor changed:

'May God give you of heaven's dew
and of earth's richness –

> *an abundance of grain and new wine.*
> *May nations serve you*
> *and peoples bow down to you.*
> *Be lord over your brothers,*
> *and may the sons of your mother*
> *bow down to you.*
> *May those who curse you be cursed*
> *and those who bless you be blessed'*
>   (Genesis 27:28–29).

Then Isaac finished his meal and Jacob retreated with a loudly beating heart to report to his mother the success of their day's work. Isaac settled himself once more to rest the rest of a satisfied man, a man who had done his duty by his God and his family.

'Away from the dew of heaven'

A shadow clouded the warm glow of his vision.

'Who's there? Who is it?' Isaac struggled to sit up.

'Esau, my father.'

'Who? Esau again?'

'No, Esau the first time. You've been dreaming, father. Look, I've brought you spiced game just as you asked.'

Isaac trembled violently.

'No, Esau, I've not been dreaming. But I can see everything clearly now. Your brother Jacob came before you and brought me spiced meat and I ate it, and I've given the Blessing of the Firstborn to Jacob, your brother.'

'Father, you can't have!'

'Yes, I have, before witnesses. He disguised himself

and disguised his voice and told me that my God had brought him quick success in the field. He has wormed his way in and has stolen your inheritance. And I can't take it back now to give it to you. It's a solemn oath. All you have left is your birthright.'

'Jacob!' bellowed Esau like a caged bull. 'Jacob is the right name for him! Swindler! Cheat! Deceiver! That's the second time. He stole my birthright and now he's taken the Blessing.'

Almost as soon as he'd said it, Esau realized that he shouldn't have mentioned the birthright. But it was too late now.

'Stole your birthright?' said Isaac. 'You never told me about that.'

Esau recounted the whole miserable story. 'But bless me, Father, as well,' he broke down, his head in his hands.

'I have given the Blessing,' said Isaac. 'There is only one. I have made him lord over you and made all his relatives his servants and promised him corn and new wine. What else is there left for you, my son?'

Esau wept and while he wept, Isaac pronounced the following prophecy:

> 'Your dwelling will be
>   away from the earth's richness,
>   away from the dew of heaven above.
> You will live by the sword
>   and you will serve your brother.
> But when you grow restless,
>   you will throw his yoke
>   from off your neck'
>   (Genesis 27:39–40).

Esau swept up the bowl of spiced meat and strode into the sunlight, blinking back the tears. Jacob, predictably, was nowhere to be seen. Esau hurled the bowl and its contents to the ground and flung himself on his own bed, his thoughts dark with murder.

It was impossible now for the brothers to live together. Esau's rage cooled to a calculated hatred. He felt that he could do nothing until Isaac died, but he vowed to himself that when that day came, and it would surely not be long now, he would be revenged on Jacob by taking his life in return for the birthright and Blessing.

The situation became rapidly obvious to the clear-sighted Rebekah and she worked out a plan to get Jacob out of the home for a few years. Much as she loved Jacob, she did not trust Esau, and preferred a distant son alive to the prospect of a corpse on the threshold of her tent.

Her plan fitted very smoothly with the family destiny. Now that Jacob was the Patriarch-elect he would need a wife. Esau had already caused uproar in the family by marrying more than one local Canaanite girl, who cared nothing for the worship of Elohim, the Creator. Rebekah reminded Isaac of this unpleasant fact, and also of their own history, and how Abraham's servant had travelled far north to Haran to find a bride for his son, Isaac, and how Rebekah herself had obeyed the summons and made the journey south.

Isaac's sense of 'family' and his own memories were touched by this approach and so it befell that it was he who sent Jacob on his way to Rebekah's home in the north.

'It would be a disaster if you did what Esau has done

40

and married one of these local infidels. Go with my blessing and find your mother's brother, Laban. Go and marry one of his daughters. I have heard that he has daughters. May the Lord make you fruitful and multiply your family. Take possession of the whole land.'

And so it was that Jacob took the second step in his career, coldly calculated, under the eye of his scheming mother. And so it was that the prophecy from his birth, 'the older will serve the younger', was fulfilled. And so it was that very early one morning Jacob kissed his mother and walked slowly to the left of the sunrise, turned once, waved his hand, and was gone.

As he walked he had ample time to reflect on that strange mixture of intrigue and destiny that seemed to be shaping his course.

- Can you parallel the scheming of Jacob and Rebekah with any recent events?
- 'Destiny' and 'luck' seem to combine to forward the materialistic careers of some people. Is there a place for God in all this?
- Where does he fit in?

—5—
Gilt-edged bonds

Jacob could well be described as a practising atheist. He believed in God, as a theory, but his life was guided by principles other than divine. What mattered to him at this early stage of his career was just that — his career: to 'better himself', 'advancement', 'prospects'. For these goals he was willing to cheat, lie and steal. If God proved useful to him, then by all means bring God into it, but not otherwise.

Nigel Rogers was not willing to cheat, lie and steal. He was an upright young man, but he also guided his life by the principle of financial betterment and material gain. He was not an atheist, but God just did not enter his calculations, literally.

One of the quirks of late twentieth-century society is the total lack of comprehension between committed Christians and those of no faith. Christians are inclined to believe that non-Christians are utterly worldly, immoral, unhappy, depressed and rootless, having no finer feelings and no love. Non-Christians see Christians as odd fanatics who practise a strange freemasonry on Sundays.

Neither seems able to understand that the difference between them, which is enormous, is not primarily moral (Christians are sinners, albeit forgiven sinners) nor a matter of feelings (non-Christians enjoy sunsets, Bach and sea-bathing just as much or as little as the faithful do). The difference is quite simply – God.

Modern secularists *assume* that there is no God. There is no debate. Whoever could imagine such a thing 'in this day and age'? Christians often feel that the secularists do believe in God really but are making excuses and running away from him. Christians know that there is a God, so this is what must be happening; secularists know that there isn't, so Christians are naïve and totally deluded. Because they start from radically dissimilar assumptions, neither side can understand the other.

A. A. Milne understood the distance that exists between two people who cannot comprehend what makes the other tick. When Pooh Bear had composed an admirable hum, he said that he supposed it just came to him. This was totally incomprehensible to Rabbit, who never waited for things to come to him, but always went and fetched them.

43

'An enormous shock'

On 8 April 1989 the *Independent Magazine* published an investigation into a religious group. The most striking point to emerge from William Dalrymple's report was this lack of understanding between the world and the believers. Dalrymple wrote, 'England is now, at root, a deeply secular society where extreme expressions of fundamentalist belief are frowned upon.'

He attended a prayer service. He writes, 'It came as an enormous shock to realize that for these people God is as real as the milkman or the bank manager.'

He realized the depth of the chasm which separated those who believe in a real God and those who do not. Most of us don't see that chasm at all. We live in a society where many church attenders are, like Jacob, practising atheists (their lives are basically ruled by self-interest), where many atheists live honourable lives, and where some whose lives *are* ruled by the real God withdraw from churches because they cannot find others there who understand them.

The confusion is compounded by politicians who support the Established Church and yet preach a 'gospel' of self-interest and materialism. So the world expects Christians to conform to the materialism of the age. They often do. But when they don't they are dismissed as harmless cranks or dangerous crack-pots.

Margaret and Gordon entertain

Margaret Barber had been getting increasingly excited and anxious about her dinner party. Gordon couldn't discover whether her excitement was stimulated more by the prospect of Nigel and Sallie or the idea of getting Gina and Bob together.

Gina Holwell was forty-six, dark-haired, vigorous and a vibrant, charismatic Christian. Some of her experiences have been recounted in *The Barnabas factor* and *The Simon Peter file*. She was a close friend of Margaret's. Margaret had helped her to see that her basic insecurity, which had shown itself in overwork and depression, had been caused by a failure properly to mourn the loss of her husband Andrew in a road accident. Gina was now much more on an even keel.

Bob Renshaw, on the other hand, was a quiet, fifty-two-year-old bachelor, living alone in one of the flats in Basingstock Road. He was another staunch member of the St Barnabas' congregation, but had caused some alarm to Cyril Kent, the only 'elder' in the church, because of his weekly visit to 'The Auld Alliance' where he kept up an acquaintance with several other middle-aged bachelors over a game of dominoes and a pint or two of ale. Cyril and Bob had talked through their differences, with Gordon's help as it happened, and each now understood the other's point of view.

It was eight o'clock. Shelley was officially in bed. Gordon was wondering whether young people in the City drank sherry before their meals and Margaret was praying – that the potatoes would soften *soon*. They'd been in for half an hour.

The front doorbell chimed.

Shelley shot out of bed and crouched on the landing, peering through the banisters to see what would happen.

Margaret dropped a spoon on the kitchen floor.

Gordon rushed to the door and opened it wide.

'OK to leave the car in the drive? Oh, right!' Sallie, wearing a brilliant red quilted jacket, black tights and high-heeled shoes, flashed a devastating smile and stepped into the hall. Nigel, in a very crisply cut black overcoat, followed, carrying a bottle.

Shelley wriggled with delight.

Gordon had wondered whether he should shake hands with Sallie. They never did at the office. Sallie, however, was kissing Margaret on both cheeks in a continental manner. Nigel also kissed Margaret on both cheeks. So this was the fashion in the City! Sallie stepped forward and kissed Gordon on both cheeks.

Gordon looked at Nigel.

Nigel looked at Gordon.

Shelley, on the landing, could contain herself no longer, gave a shriek of mirth, hastily stifled with a handkerchief, and in the ensuing chaos, while she was allowed to be introduced, Gordon and Nigel shook hands and decided what to do with the bottle.

Into this melée Gina Holwell arrived and there was more continental kissing before the company agreed that sherry would be very acceptable and after all they weren't in the City now. Margaret thought that Gina's narrow black skirt and lace-fronted blouse were very appropriate to the occasion. When Sallie removed her jacket she revealed a short woollen garment with a neckline too low for Gordon's spiritual health, in Margaret's opinion, and she seemed to have forgotten her skirt. Gordon, however, didn't seem to mind.

Nigel's immaculate suit certainly made Gordon's tweed sports jacket look twenty years old (which it was), but when Bob appeared, wearing a faded green turtle-necked sweater and baggy grey flannels,

Margaret gave up in despair and retired to the kitchen to see whether her prayer had been answered.

A big step forward?

The meal over, conversation turned to problems encountered at work. Gina worked in the Council offices at Canford Heath and had stories to tell about red tape and the public services. Bob was an inspector, working for the London Underground, where his job was to ensure that signalling systems were functioning properly. Nobody present had heard Bob talk about his work before and everyone was impressed by the responsibility he shouldered and the calm and matter-of-fact way he approached it.

Sallie and Gordon compared notes on work for Drew, Drew & Drew, while Margaret, recognizing that as a full-time mother and housewife she had little to contribute to this conversation, kept herself busy replenishing coffee cups and asking the right questions.

Meanwhile Nigel was sitting silently, half listening to the others and half occupied by his own thoughts. At length he took the opportunity of a pause in the flow of talk.

'It's an odd coincidence that we're talking about work problems because I've got one and perhaps some of you people can help me with it.'

'Nigel, you never told me,' said Sallie.

'Well, it's only come up finally today and we haven't had time to discuss it.' There was a long pause. 'I suppose I know what you'll say, but let me tell you anyway.

'My boss has asked me to head up the marketing of a new gilt-edged bonds issue. It's the kind of investment

47

that will appeal to people with some savings, middle-aged people with two jobs going in the family, pensioners perhaps, people who have been left money by their parents. The brochures make it seem like a cast-iron certainty. It will be well subscribed. I stand to take quite a big step forward if I can make it work.'

'Nige, that's great!' said Sallie admiringly.

'But,' said Gordon, 'there's a "but", isn't there?'

'Yes, there is. I'm not certain that the offer is as gilt-edged as it looks.'

'But people have been badly caught out by this sort of thing several times in the last year or two,' said Sallie. 'They'll only put their money in it if *they're* certain. It's a case of *caveat emptor*.'

'Yer what?' said Bob.

'*Caveat emptor*. Buyer beware. "It's not *my* fault if you buy a load of dud bonds." See what I mean?'

Bob nodded.

'No, but it could be mine,' said Nigel. 'I'm the one who persuades them that there is no risk whatever, that they'll be in clover for the rest of their lives.'

'And you don't fully believe it,' said Gordon.

'Well, of course, in a situation like this you can never be absolutely certain. There's always some risk. But in this case it looks as if my boss is going to use the money raised to speculate in high-risk shares. Our publicity says that it will be invested in safe gilts. Shall I say that *I* wouldn't buy the bonds but I have to persuade OAPs to buy them.'

'What would happen if you refused to do it?' asked Gordon.

'There are plenty of other people with their names down for my office,' said Nigel gloomily.

'Nigel!' Sallie was looking thoroughly alarmed.

'Well, my colleagues are not all my friends. And my boss certainly isn't.'

'Why has he given the job to you then?' asked Gina.

'Probably because he doesn't like me. And if it goes wrong. . .chop!'

'Well, I think you've got no choice. Go for it, Nige, and win!' Sallie was in no doubt.

'Since you've asked our opinion,' said Gina, '*I* would say don't touch it.'

'And what about his job?'

'*I* would say that the Lord will provide.'

'How much does the Lord pay monthly and is there a pension?'

Gordon felt that some diplomacy was needed at this point and so he steered the conversation into more peaceful waters. Nigel obviously had a lively conscience already and Gina did go over the top a bit sometimes. The evening finished on a more positive note, the guests went home happily and even Nigel seemed to have cheered up.

Throughout the washing-up, which was fairly extensive, Margaret remained strangely preoccupied. Gordon made several attempts to extract her opinion about the Crieff-Farbsteen business, but although she made sensible replies there was no discussion or conclusion.

Gordon went to the back door to check the milk order and lock up. When he returned he heard a strange shuffling and clicking sound from the hall. He was astonished to see his usually quiet and even staid wife waltzing round the hall with an imaginary partner.

'Margaret! Good grief!' said Gordon.

'He walked home with Gina!' said Margaret gleefully.

'Well, it was the polite thing to do.'

'Sallie offered her a lift as they were going her way and she *refused*!'

'Have you ever sat in the back seat of a TR7?'

'Gordon, don't be so unro*man*tic! Bob lives in exactly the opposite direction. He'll have a mile and a half to walk back. Don't you think he'd be good for her?'

'I don't know,' said Gordon. 'Here's Nigel Rogers who has to gamble with his well-paid job or else risk the small fortunes of hundreds of people and all you think about is matchmaking. You should have been called England's Glory.'

The rest of the conversation is not recorded, but a few minutes later when Shelley had been awakened by voices and peered down into the hall she was astonished to see both her parents dancing silently round it.

She crept back to bed with a look of wonder in her eyes. 'Good grief!' was all she said.

- ■ What is your belief about the existence of God?
  - – definitely not?
  - – could be?
  - – yes, but it doesn't really make much difference?
  - – definitely yes, he governs my life?
- ■ Does this matter need more thinking about?

6

The St Barnabas' appeal

Mrs Goodrich had a telephone beside her bed. She was ninety-six and never left her bed, so the telephone was her only link with the outside world. Well, there was Jane, of course. Jane was her only daughter and Jane devoted herself almost entirely to looking after her mother. Increasingly troubled with arthritis and now sixty-four, Jane was imprisoned by her mother's incapacity, and she lived under her domination. As a member of the St Barnabas' church council she did have that one other occupation, which saved her from total collapse.

Mrs Goodrich was now involved in a long conversation with Mrs Beesley. Mrs Beesley was a youngster of seventy-six who lived at 'The Haven'.

51

She rarely visited the Goodrich home, 64 Fairview Avenue ('Nobody *ever* visits me!'), but was a useful channel for local information. This time Mrs Goodrich had some information and was making the most of it.

'Last night, yes dear, last night. . .Getting on for midnight I should think. . .No, I don't know who he was. It was dark you know. He hadn't got a car. Well, they were walking. . .No. He didn't go inside, at least I don't think so. But they were talking for a long time before he went.'

Gina Holwell lived at number 67 Fairview Avenue, under the constant gaze of Mrs Goodrich round the edge of her drawn curtains.

Mrs Beesley also had information.

'I happen to know that Gina Holwell went to the Barbers' for supper last night. . .No, I know it wasn't Gordon Barber who took her home. We don't want to start that one all over again, but they had those new people, you know, the couple who live together and aren't married. They had them to supper as well. . .No, it wasn't them taking Gina home either. Listen. It was Bob Renshaw. Bob Renshaw from the flats in Basingstock Road. . .I know because Connie Bassett told me. . .*She* knew because she was with them in church when they fixed it up. Isn't that interesting. . .?'

And so the wheels of the local communication industry rolled into action and the names of Gina Holwell and Bob Renshaw began to be linked. Villages, they say, are where everyone knows everyone else's business. Those who make such exclusive claims should live for a while in a London suburb.

How were they to pay for it?

Jane Goodrich sighed deeply as she closed her front
door and wheeled her shopping trolley down the path.
She tried not to listen to her mother's conversations, of
course, but she couldn't help hearing the name of Gina
Holwell. Poor Gina. She always acted from the best
motives, but so often things went wrong, and always
there was mother, peeping from behind her curtain to
report on the action.

There was that time two years ago when mother
had started a scandal because Gina had been seen
with Gordon Barber (*The Barnabas factor*, chapter
six). Then last year Gina had had too much to
drink at a party and had to be brought home by
the police (*The Simon Peter file*, chapter seven).
Mother wasn't the only one who knew about that.
And now something else. . .As she reached the end
of Fairview Avenue and turned into Highwood Avenue
towards the shops, Jane saw Cyril and Edith Kent, also
bound for Food Fayre, so she crossed the road and
joined them.

Cyril was now seventy-nine, a stolid supporter of
the established order of things, especially in church.
He had been an implacable opponent of change in
the church's forms of worship, change proposed and
vigorously pursued by the ebullient Gina Holwell.
There had been a great debate about removing pews
and substituting chairs, converting the church to an
octagonal form with the holy table in the middle.
In the end he had agreed to the move, though, at
first, without enthusiasm. A number of influences

had changed Cyril's outlook on life. Gordon Barber had gone out of his way to be encouraging. Connie Bassett had come to Cyril for baptism preparation, someone so unlike him as to cause great hilarity, but she had been like a gust of new air in the Kent household. Then there was the strange affair of Cyril's boil that had mysteriously disappeared while a healing service was going on at church. Odd, that.

So Cyril had joined the general euphoria, as it now seemed, as the church voted unanimously to change its layout and while they were about it, build a new kitchen and toilet extension, with a meeting room, which would link the church to the church hall. As a solution to the debate it pleased everyone because the church could still be used in its old way if the chairs were moved, and a sense of unity had bridged the gap between the old conservatives and the younger progressives. Gordon Barber's plan for the new layout had solved all their problems. Except one. How were they to pay for it?

Cyril had been talking to Gordon and had advance news of the architect's estimate. How much did Jane think? Jane had no idea about these things but she supposed you could not get a house under a hundred thousand pounds in Canwell Park these days, so — seventy-five thousand?

Cyril paused before he spoke again.

'Three. Hundred. And fifty-five. Thousand,' he said impressively.

'Oh, Cyril!' gasped Edith admiringly. She had already heard the figure but she always said, 'Oh, Cyril!'

admiringly, whenever her husband spoke with that kind of impressiveness.

'We can't possibly afford it, of course. It puts a new complexion on the whole business.'

Jane wasn't so sure.

'If it's the right thing for us to do, and we believed it was, then the money will come in,' said Jane. 'Books have been written about churches in just this kind of situation, and not only has God provided them with the money, but the working and giving together has drawn them into a stronger fellowship.'

'I don't doubt that God could provide the money,' said Cyril. 'We all know about George Müller in Bristol and how God supplied his children's homes through faith. God *could* do it for us. But the question is, "Does God *want* us to spend that sort of money on this sort of project?" It looks very much like making ourselves comfortable in our own little nest while half the world's population is starving to death.'

'Oh, Cyril!' said Edith.

'I suppose that's true,' said Jane thoughtfully. 'But we're not likely to raise £350,000 to feed the world's hungry, are we? The choice is between doing nothing and going ahead with our building. But I'm sure you agree that the money is not ours to do what we like with. It's God's isn't it? "All things come from you and of your own do we give you."'

And there the subject was dropped as all their concentration was needed to cross High Road by the War Memorial and to plunge into the maelstrom of Food Fayre.

'What do they get out of it?'

Nigel and Sallie were returning from their second experience of a service at St Barnabas' church.

They had met Gina and Bob again. Those two seemed to be linked in their minds now. Well, they had sat together during the service. And Connie Bassett. You couldn't avoid meeting her. And they had met the Jenkins family. Fred, the one who always raised his arms during the choruses of hymns, and his wife Joan who looked embarrassed whenever he did it. A nice couple, though. Daughter Carol was away at university now, Fred told them, doing great things in the Christian Union. Joan had looked embarrassed again.

The great news on that Sunday was that Diana Monteith was going to have a baby. Her first! At thirty-six! There was much talk after the service and great rejoicing all round.

The weather being fine, Nigel had suggested that they walk to church, much to Sallie's surprise as Nigel rarely walked anywhere. So they found themselves in the sunshine, walking between the row of poplars that skirted the tennis club grounds and the little River Can as it flowed across Canwell Park on its way to join another river, only ten miles to the north, a larger river and better known.

Nigel and Sallie reflected on the church as they had seen it thus far.

'What are they in it for?' Nigel was asking. 'What do they get out of it?'

'I think some of them would say that's the wrong question,' said Sallie.

'But you're bound to have a reason for being͕ or a church or a building society or you wouldn't be in it at all. And the reason must be an advantage for you. Even if they think they're getting to heaven, that's a calculation of what they get out of it.'

'Pie in the sky when you die.'

'Yes, but there's more pie before then, isn't there? It's a small world of about two hundred people at most and you can *be* somebody if your world's that small. Those people who take the collection plates round and march up to the front with them. As proud as punch they are. Churchwardens they have, and church council members: and an elder. Cyril Kent his name is. A dry old stick. But they're all somebodies. And Timothy Monteith is the Big Somebody. They almost worship him.'

'You seem to know a lot all of a sudden.'

'Yes, I was talking to Bob Renshaw. He's a quiet sort of guy, isn't he? No ambitions there.'

'So what does he get out of church?'

'I suppose it satisfies his conscience. He said he feels empty if he doesn't go to church once a week. It becomes a habit, a kind of drug. And you can't escape from it.'

'They enjoy it though, don't they? It's not just a duty.'

'Yes, there's another advantage. If you enjoy something you'll go on doing it. And it's harmless.'

'It's harmless enough,' said Sallie, 'but it's very expensive.'

'What, a quid on the plate every week?'

'Three hundred and fifty grand to rebuild the church!'

'Three hundred and fifty! Wowee! Who've you been talking to?'

'Gordon.'

'Oh yes, you accountants do attract one another. But that's more than. . .that's nearly two thousand *each*!'

'Yup.'

'How do they propose to get that much?'

'Don't know yet. They have a meeting next week.'

'Well, if they're thinking of money-raising at that sort of level, they must think the whole thing is worthwhile,' said Nigel, ready to be impressed, despite himself.

'And it's not just that. There's *something* about them.' Sallie was almost at a loss for words. 'When they hold hands and smile at one another, it brings a lump into your throat.'

'*Your* throat.'

'OK, my throat. But they really do believe that Jesus came back to life, you know.'

'They don't!'

'They do. I thought it was only the Born Again people and Billy Graham who believed that sort of thing, but these people do as well.'

'But this is the Church of England. The Bishop of Durham says. . .'

'They don't agree with the Bishop of Durham,' said Sallie firmly. 'Timothy told me. But whatever difference it can possibly make two thousand years later I can't imagine. I mean, this is nearly the twenty-first century.'

'Talking of which,' said Nigel, 'people are going to find out about this church-going of ours. It's not going to be very easy in the office if it gets out. Just imagine what old Hogwood will say for starters: "Our young entrepreneur appears to have 'got religion', gentlemen. If he sells more shares than you do, don't be surprised. It's because he prays to succeed. He has God on his side now, so you others don't have a – chance. Haw, haw, haw!"'

'So the church is going to be no advantage to *us*, is it, darling?'

'I never thought it would be. It's only a marriage of convenience, in more senses than one.'

'Unless of course, there *is* something in this prayer business?'

'What do you mean?'

'They all believe it works.'

'Well?'

'That's another reason for being a Christian. Having God on your side. Perhaps it does work, you know.'

'He certainly would be a powerful ally just now,' said Nigel as he fitted his key into the front door lock. 'We could do with a prayer or two.'

■ Why do you think people go to church?
■ Why do you (or why don't you)?
■ Which are the right reasons and which are the wrong ones?

7

Appointment with God

Starting out on a journey stirs the depths of human feelings. There's something mystical about fresh beginnings, new leaves, the open road. Many are the stories and legends which see a journey as a powerful picture of life itself, notably *The Pilgrim's Progress*. More frequently read nowadays is Tolkien's *Lord of the Rings*, containing that haunting poem:

The Road goes ever on and on
  Down from the door where it began.
Now far ahead the Road has gone,
  And I must follow if I can,
Pursuing it with eager feet,
  Until it joins some larger way

Where many paths and errands meet.
*And whither then? I cannot say.**

Feelings like these, a mixture of high excitement, some trepidation and a sense of destiny, must have run strongly in Jacob's mind as he trudged on his way towards Haran. His old life of frustration and idleness was behind him and he had secured the inheritance and the spiritual privileges of the head of the tribe. What lay ahead? Adventure certainly. Marriage? Advancement. Prospects. Success. Security.

'Jacob left Beersheba and set out for Haran', states Genesis 28:10 simply enough, and goes on to describe a remarkable dream and Jacob's characteristic response, which could well be labelled an appointment with God.

Staircase to heaven

The freshness of the morning and the high hopes of starting soon give way to the glare of midday and the dust of the road. Suddenly the prospects look less inviting. Doubt creeps in as feet become sore and legs weary.

Jacob had no plans for bed and breakfast. He went on walking each day until he could walk no further. On the second or third night, 'When he reached a certain place, he stopped. . .because the sun had set' (Genesis 28:11). He had no camping equipment with him. Was he alone, or had he a faithful servant? The story does not tell. But he was vulnerable, sleeping in a strange part of the country with a stone for a pillow. A stone? Total weariness does not demand feathers.

*J. R. R. Tolkien, *The Fellowship of the Ring* (Unwin Hyman, p.44, reproduced by permission).

Perhaps the ground was hard and his choice of pillow too spartan, so Jacob's sleep was not dreamless. In fact he dreamed a spectacular dream. He saw a stairway, starting from the ground nearby and stretching up and up until it reached heaven itself. As he watched, bright and shining ones ascended and descended the stairway, clearly doing business that concerned both heaven and earth.

More was yet to be revealed. As Jacob followed the ascending bright beings with his gaze he saw, standing high above them all, One who could only be God himself. And God was speaking to him:

> *'I am the LORD, the God of your father Abraham and the God of Isaac. I will give you and your descendants the land on which you are lying. Your descendants will be like the dust of the earth, and you will spread out to the west and to the east, to the north and to the south. All peoples on earth will be blessed through you and your offspring. I am with you and will watch over you wherever you go, and I will bring you back to this land. I will not leave you'*
> (Genesis 28:13–15).

Jacob awoke. And it was all a dream. But what a dream! One of those dreams in which every detail is finely chiselled in the memory and which leaves an overwhelming sense of being more real than waking reality.

Fully awake now, under the brilliant stars of Canaan Jacob went over and over the dream, repeating the words until they were fixed in his mind. And as he did so he became aware that the dream had been more than a mental picture show.

'Surely the Lord is in this place,' he thought, 'and I hadn't realized it.'

God had been far from his thoughts. God did not usually feature dramatically in Jacob's reckoning, but he must have been so powerfully present as to penetrate the sleeper's inmost imaginings. He felt a sudden surge of fear.

'How awesome this place is. This is none other than the house of God; this is the gate of heaven.'

He slept again, dreaming no more but deeply conscious that he was not alone and that his Companion was not to be trifled with.

Fair's fair

Jacob awoke refreshed. The sun was up but the morning was still cool. He stretched himself, washed in the clear water of the spring he had seen last night and set about preparing breakfast.

Only then did he remember with a shock his dream. How could he have forgotten? The impact of it all, the very words of the promise, came back to him.

But wait a bit! It was morning. A breeze was blowing. Everything stood out clearly in the level light of the rising sun. Jacob looked around. The place where he had seen the stairway so firmly fixed to the ground was now a patch of grass and scrubby bushes. No sign of a stairway there. The power of the dream began to fade. Reality was the here and now, with a new day dawning.

On the other hand it would be better not to take any chances. Jacob was no fool. If there was anything in all this promising to be with him and so on, it would be better to keep on the right side of any God there might be around.

So Jacob looked for a suitable memorial. His stone pillow had probably caused him to dream the dream so it would be symbolic to use that. He set it up on end in the ground and poured a little cooking oil on the top of it.

'This is now Beth-el, house of God,' said Jacob aloud. 'And this pillar shall be its foundation stone.'

This didn't seem quite enough somehow. He thought perhaps he had better pray as well, just to make everything proper. And as he considered the form that his prayer might take he remembered what God had promised him in the dream. If God was going to do all that for him then he would hold him to it. He would remind God of all that he had promised and strike a bargain. If God would stand by his promises (*if* he had made any), then Jacob was ready to fulfil his part of the bargain.

So Jacob stood by his pillar which had recently been a pillow, and up to that point of history had lain unnoticed for thousands of years, and made this vow:

'*If* God will be with me;
'*If* God will watch over me on this journey;
'*If* God will give me food to eat;
'*If* God will give me clothes to wear;
'*If* God will bring me safely back to my father's house; then that God, who can give me all that I want and need, shall be my God.'

In his concern for his own safety, Jacob forgot the dimensions of destiny, his future offspring, the spreading of his people to the four corners of the earth, the blessing of the nations. These things were

God's concerns perhaps, but they did not immediately trouble Jacob.

Now came the big moment. Jacob had to promise something to God. If God was going to do all this for him, he must promise something dramatic in return. Dramatic yes, but not too dramatic. Jacob was a careful calculator and a shrewd businessman, even in the presence of God. He quickly worked out what seemed to him to be a good rate of interest on the investment God was offering him and prayed this prayer:

'This stone that I have set up as a pillar will be God's house, and of all that you give me I will give you a tenth' (Genesis 28:22).

This last phrase was the only part of the whole prayer to be addressed directly to God. It is very short, almost breathless, as if he hoped that God might not hear it, or if he heard it, soon forget.

Whether God was pleased with the bargain or whether he smiled a knowing divine smile we are not told, but it was a beginning. It was probably the first real encounter with God that Jacob had ever experienced.

Shelley Barber advises

'5742. . .Yes, this is Shelley speaking. . .hello, Nigel. . . yes, thank you. . .oh, do you like "Catatonic State"? They're down to twenty-five in this week's charts. They can't sustain the vocals. . .

'Daddy's out. He won't be very long. . .Mummy's washing her hair.'

'Oh well, not to worry,' said Nigel, preparing to ring off. 'I just wanted to discuss something with your dad.'

'Is it about your bonds and the old people?'

There was an astonished pause.

'What do you know about bonds and old people?' said Nigel guardedly.

'Oh, your boss wants you to sell them but the old people ought not to buy them because they're not worth it and it might be unkind to the old people.'

'I don't think your daddy ought to have discussed my affairs in front of you.'

'Oh no, he didn't. He's very discreet.'

Nigel laughed in spite of himself.

'That's a big word for a seven-year-old.'

'Eight,' said Shelley firmly. 'But I heard you telling everyone about your bonds last week when you came to supper. My bedroom is above the sitting room and the chimney goes up behind my bed so if I lie very still and if people talk loud enough I can hear what they say. And you,' she ended simply, 'talk loud enough.'

'I'll remember that in future,' said Nigel. 'So what do you think I should do about my problem?'

'Pray about it, of course.'

There was another silence.

'What do you mean, Shelley?'

'I mean, pray. Ask God to show you what to do. He does. I had to decide whether to go to a party or a Sunday School thing' (Nigel wisely forbore to ask what the 'thing' was in case the explanation took too long) 'and I prayed and the Sunday School teacher fell down and broke her ankle so I could go to the party.'

Nigel stuffed his handkerchief into his mouth and there was another pause. At that moment Margaret Barber emerged from the bathroom wearing a towel. Fearing the worst she snatched the telephone from

Shelley's unwilling grasp and heard Nigel's version of the conversation.

'Your daughter appears to believe that the Almighty will intervene in this matter,' said Nigel, 'but I don't want to be the indirect cause of broken ankles.'

'I think you can safely leave that part of it to God,' laughed Margaret, 'but it's always worth a try, isn't it? You can't do any harm by discussing it with him.'

'But where is he? I can't dial G.O.D. on the 'phone.'

'Well, remember what Jacob said.'

'Jacob who?'

'Sorry, I mean Jacob in the Bible – "Surely God is in this place and I hadn't realized it." He's everywhere, so you can call at any time.'

'You people do astonish me,' said Nigel. 'You really believe that, don't you?'

'Why not?' said Margaret. 'But look, Nigel, I'm beginning to get cold and I'm sure you should talk to Gordon about this one. He'll be in at about seven.'

'I think I've got enough to be going on with,' said Nigel. 'Tell Shelley I'll take her advice and see what happens.'

'What did he say, Mummy?' asked Shelley.

'He said he'll take your advice,' said Margaret, disappearing into the bathroom.

'Good,' said Shelley, happily. 'I think he should too.'

- Has God ever appeared to you, or anyone you know, in a dream?
- If he did, how seriously would you take it?
- How else is he contactable?

8

'Can I have a word with you, Gordon?'

Sunday lunchtime at the Barbers' was usually a relaxed affair. On the whole, Sunday was not a day of rest for Gordon or Margaret – both had heavy responsibilities at St Barnabas' – and Shelley threw herself into the morning class with her usual total commitment. So lunchtime was a breathing-space, when the family could 'centre down', as Margaret liked to put it.

Today, however, looked like being an exception. Gordon was under siege. He had been approached immediately after the morning service by Bob Renshaw. 'Can I have a word with you, Gordon?' After seeing the morning collection into the church safe and arriving home half an hour late, he had been telephoned by a very anxious Jane Goodrich about the church building fund. 'Can I have a word with you, Gordon?'

'If anyone else says, "Can I have a word with you, Gordon?" I think I shall scream,' said Gordon as he replaced the receiver.

Shelley looked interested. 'Do you think you could?' she said, 'I mean, a proper one. Try.'

Gordon uttered a feeble yelp, but before Shelley could take him properly in hand and teach him screaming as it really should be done, Margaret called all hands to help and their time for relaxing had begun. Gordon had picked up the gravy jug to help Shelley when the 'phone rang again.

'Can I have a word with you, Gordon?' cried Shelley gleefully, and risked having the gravy poured over her head.

'Let it ring,' said Margaret. So they did. And it did. In the end Gordon could stand it no longer and gave in. He picked up the receiver, paused, put his hand over it and yelped again. After a brief pause he was back.

'What time do yuppies eat?' Gordon returned to the gravy.

'Was that Sallie?'

'Nigel. "Can I have a word with you, Gordon?"'

'Oh, they'll have finished,' said Margaret. 'They go to the carvery on Sundays.'

'What's a carvery, Mummy?' asked Shelley.

'A place where you go and eat well and pay through the nose,' said Gordon.

'Yuk!' said Shelley, disgusted.

'Anyway, I'll call him back later. Now let's enjoy our own private carvery.'

'Where we don't pay at all,' observed Shelley.

'Well. . .' said Gordon. 'Oh, never mind. I've had

69

enough problems for one day.'

Trotting along behind

The first of the problems had been Bob Renshaw's.

'I'm sorry to mention it now, just when you're counting the collection and all, but I need your advice. It won't take a minute.'

'My advice doesn't usually last as long as that,' said Gordon cheerfully. 'Advice about what then?'

'Gina Holwell.'

'Aha!'

'We've been seeing each other quite a bit recently.'

'That's nice.'

'Oh yes. I'm not complaining, but I, er, we, have to decide whether we should go on or not.'

'And you want my advice,' said Gordon.

'Yes, I think I can rely on you to be unbiased.'

'Well, it's not for me to tell you what to do. You're of age, you know. What are the pros and cons as you see them?'

'There are a lot of cons, I think. Gina's been married before and Andrew was a mate of the Archangel Gabriel from the way she talks about him. I'd never match up to him and I think I should be compared with him all the time. And I've been a bachelor all my life. I don't think it would be very easy to change gear at this stage.'

'It has happened before now,' said Gordon, 'but go on.'

'Then there's the spiritual dimension – that's what Gina calls it. My faith is a simple matter – you know, trust in Christ for salvation, love God and do what you can to help people. But Gina's into this charismatic business, and going to big conventions and lots of prayer and Bible reading and what not. I haven't got that kind of strength. I'd be afraid of trotting along behind her all the time, trying to keep up.'

'There are three cons,' said Gordon, 'that's enough to be going on with. What about the pros?'

'That's the problem, really,' said Bob, looking round the church as if for information. 'Apart from the fact that we get on well together and are glad of the companionship, there aren't any obvious positive points at all.' He looked at Gordon helplessly like a dog with a thorn in its paw.

'It's not quite so simple, is it?' said Gordon. 'I mean, from what I've just heard you have three good reasons against and one fairly average one in favour. Simple. Give up. But,' Gordon waved his hand as Bob tried to interrupt, 'but I can see that it's a bit more than "getting on well", isn't it? There's a pretty strong attraction, isn't there?'

'Well, yes. I suppose if I was thirty years younger I'd say that I'd fallen in love with her. It's very odd. We've known each other at a distance for years, but it was that evening at your house. Gina seemed so secure and comfortable compared with those two young people with all their wild ideas and blatant. . .'

'Materialism?'

'Yes, materialism. Yes, the more I get to know Gina the more I admire her faith. She seems to have things in proportion.'

'She's been through an awful lot, you know.'

'Yes, that's another problem. I've trundled along through life with very few ups and downs and she's so. . .mature.'

71

'What does Gina think about you?'

There was a long pause.

'She seems to like me, or she wouldn't go on seeing me.'

'I mean, what does she think about your being suited to one another?'

'I don't know,' said Bob miserably. 'She won't say. I think she's afraid of making me feel inferior. That's another thing. I've just said "inferior". It's a posh kind of Gina word. She's got a lot more words than I have. She's been to university. But I don't think she knows what to think, really. She's going to see Margaret and ask her what she thinks.'

'Margaret!' Gordon started.

'Well, they're as thick as thieves.'

'That's just it,' said Gordon. 'She won't get a balanced and unbiased view from Margaret. My wife is an incurable matchmaker.'

'I thought she'd done a counselling course. They teach them to be unbiased, don't they?'

'Oh yes,' said Gordon, 'they do. But in this case I don't know whether Margaret the counsellor or Margaret the matchmaker will win.'

Gordon set off home, determined to talk to Margaret about this one before Gina did. But as soon as he set foot in the house, the 'phone rang and Jane's troubled voice said, 'Gordon, can I have a word with you?'

'You do see my problem, don't you?'

Jane sounded tearful. She suffered from arthritis, loneliness and her mother and was frequently tearful.

72

'Jane, what is it?' Gordon forgot Bob and Gina in a moment.

'It's the appeal,' said Jane. 'All that money. I've hardly slept for a week.'

'But it's not your decision, on your own. It's for the steering committee to decide. We shall pray about it and take a vote and go the way we all believe the Lord is leading us. You don't need to worry about it, Jane.'

'But I do, Gordon. I have to vote, haven't I? And I don't know which way to vote.'

'Well,' said Gordon, 'why don't you weigh up the pros and cons?' (wondering how many more pros and cons there would be that day).

'You know I have been against the idea of the change all along. I like the old pews as they are. I very much dislike chairs in church and I don't like the idea of music groups and dance and drama and all that kind of thing. And I think that £350,000 is far too much to expect us to raise and that it will distract us from what we should be doing.'

'You've been talking to Cyril,' said Gordon gently.

'Well, yes, I have. I told him that God could provide the money for us if he wanted to, but I do agree with him that God may not wish us to do it.'

'Then, vote against the scheme,' said Gordon.

'But I should have to vote against all my friends,' said Jane dismally. 'Gina has been so good, you know, and it was her idea to start with. And Timothy, he's such a dear and so keen to go ahead. And the scheme as we've got it now is yours. How can I vote against all you good people? How can I be right and all of you be wrong? You do see my problem, don't you?'

Gordon did see her problem and did his best to help her to see it in perspective. As church treasurer and author of the proposal himself he was not an unbiased observer and, although he did not admit it to anyone but Margaret, was deeply troubled about the whole thing himself. For this reason his words of comfort seemed to lack conviction, but Jane was happy to have spoken to him and said goodbye with a firmer voice.

The power of the City

And now for Nigel. Gordon soon realized that his Sunday afternoon off was evaporating and that he would need to discuss Nigel's problem face to face rather than by telephone, so he left Margaret and Shelley as soon as the washing-up was done and walked to Canwell Gardens.

'I'm collecting a few opinions, you see,' said Nigel, when they were comfortably sunk in their armchairs. 'You've got some pretty good ideas about the market.'

'Well, you yourself said you wouldn't invest your own money in it,' said Gordon. 'It can't be all that safe.'

'No, I mean safe for *me*,' said Nigel. 'I know it's not 100% sure for the investors. As I said before, these things never are. But if it all blows up and there's a crash, I shall be in the middle of it.'

'Besides which,' said Sallie, who had so far taken no part in the conversation but had been posing decoratively on the hearthrug, 'a lot of people who will buy these shares will be the clients of Drew, Drew & Drew. Whose side am I supposed to be on?'

Gordon saw the point, but tried to remain neutral.

'If you're asking my opinion, as a private individual and as a Christian, I have to ask you to consider whether what you're proposing to do is ethical. Is it in line with what is *right*?'

'I didn't ask you here to give me a lecture on morals,' said Nigel loudly. 'How can *you* know what's right, anyway? Right is surely what happens in the end.'

'No, right, as I see it, is what is in line with God's will, as revealed in the Bible.'

'The Bible? But that's the culture textbook of a sect of Jews 2,000 years ago! They didn't know anything about the stock market and investment and all that!'

'I think if you were to read the Bible carefully you'd find a lot about money and its use,' said Gordon, 'but of course it's the principles that have to be applied to our own situation.'

'Do they?' said Nigel. 'Well, if you compare the power of the City, the sheer weight of economic forces moving round the world at the flick of a switch, with the mutterings of a few holy men dressed in blankets and tea-towels, you'd hesitate to bring all this God-talk into it. I don't think your advice is going to help me much.'

'Nigel,' said Sallie, 'aren't you going a bit over the top? Gordon's doing his best to answer your question.'

'Sorry,' said Nigel. 'OK. But we just don't see things from the same angle.'

And there the subject was dropped for the time being. As Gordon walked home he reflected on how very far apart their ideas seemed to be. And, if Nigel and Sallie were involved with the church now, how diametrically opposed their materialist views were to the kingdom of God. And he began to wonder how many other good church attenders were, deep down, as materialistic as that. He began to wonder about himself. . .

On the other hand, Nigel did seem to flare up in defence of his own views in an exaggerated way. Did he really feel secure or was his conscience troubling him? It was the same with his living with Sallie. He defended it often and irritably. Perhaps he was unsure about that too, deep down.

As Gordon reached home again, the 'phone was ringing. Margaret answered it.

'Margaret, Gina here. Can I have a word with you?'

Gordon took the hint as Margaret motioned him to go away. He shut himself in the kitchen and reached for the teapot.

■ Are you good at listening to people's problems?

■ Do you try to solve them or just listen?

9

Jacob takes a dose of medicine

The sun seemed to be directly overhead. The searing heat pressed on Jacob's head and shoulders. Perspiration was running down his face. He made a mental note that he would never travel in the heat of the day again. Up till now he had moved in the early morning and found shade at midday, but after thirty days' walking he was aware that he must be near to Haran, the home of his uncle Laban. So he kept going in the hope of reaching civilization that day.

In fact he had travelled with more hope than he could have imagined. The dream of the stairway and his vow to God had given him a sense of destiny. Someone, somewhere, was on his side. Jacob was retracing the steps of his ancestors, as well as his grandfather's servant, and felt that he was in the mainstream of history.

At this particular moment, however, he wished that he was under a palm tree instead. The heat was getting unbearable.

Brown eyes

Jacob became aware of the bleating of sheep. For some reason flocks were gathering round what was obviously a well. If the sheep could drink, so could he, and anyway the shepherds might give him information.

But when he came near to the well he could see that the stone lid was firmly in place and the shepherds seemed to be waiting for something. Perhaps, thought Jacob, they were waiting for him. His time had come.

'My brothers,' he said, 'where are you from?'

'Haran.'

'Then my journey is almost over. Do you know Laban, Nahor's grandson?'

'Yes, we know him.'

'Is he well?'

'Yes, he is.'

These country folk were not great conversationalists. Jacob was surprised when one of them offered more information.

'See that flock yonder? That's Rachel, Laban's daughter, with her sheep.'

'What's going on here?' asked Jacob. 'Have you come to water the sheep? If so, why don't you get on with it?'

His new companions opened their eyes wide in astonishment.

78

'There are but three flocks here.'

'So?'

'We *never* open the well until the fourth comes. *Then* we can roll the stone away.'

This was clearly some unwritten rule. What strange people they were. In any case it was too early to gather the sheep, not much past midday. Jacob voiced his thoughts.

'No, we'll go back to pasture after watering. We have to water twice a day hereabouts. No surface water to be had.'

But Jacob wasn't listening. He was gazing into the largest and most beautiful brown eyes he had ever seen. Regardless of offending local custom, he rolled away the well-stone himself and drew water for his uncle's sheep. Rachel's eyes, in a moment of time, had made him more selfless than a lifetime of religion.

Rachel had no idea who this man was, acting in this odd manner. Suddenly, to her alarm, he strode across to her and kissed her and announced that he was her aunt Rebekah's son. As if that was not enough shock for one day, this dishevelled, perspiring stranger burst into tears. Rachel left her sheep where they were and ran. . .

Later that day, in the shade of Laban's portico, everything was explained and it was arranged that Jacob would stay with the family for a while and work for Laban in return for board and lodging. Jacob only half heard what Laban was saying. He could not take his eyes off Rachel. This girl had a graceful body as well as lovely eyes. He, Jacob, actually agreed to work for someone else without fixing a wage. He was in love already. And her father was rich, so rich. Perhaps God meant what he had said after all.

Love on probation

Jacob had lost his moorings. In the first place, he had never been away from home before and the effort of looking after himself and finding his way over 450 miles of unknown terrain had been very great. His meeting with God in the dream at Bethel had knocked him sideways and his encounter with these strange country folk with their laconic replies, odd customs and stubborn attitudes confused him. And now Rachel. . .

How he longed for Rachel. That first kiss was not repeated. In the tightly organized settlement the women had their quarters and kept to their own tasks. Neither did he see more of Rachel than her eyes and the tantalizing hints of her shapely body hidden by the folds of her robes. But the eyes seemed to return his approval and the the occasional words that they were able to exchange showed Jacob that he was not unwelcome. And he had a vivid imagination. How he longed for Rachel.

It seemed but a few days later, but was in reality a month, when Laban called Jacob to him. He was anxious to put their relationship on a well-defined footing, so, in typical middle-eastern fashion he opened the bargaining with what sounded like a generous offer, which he expected to be refused.

'Jacob, my son. You really mustn't be so naïve as to work for me for no wages. If you're going to stay here with us you must name your figure and you shall have it.'

The only figure Jacob had in mind was Rachel's.

'Look, Laban, I'm not interested in money just now. What I want most in the world is your daughter. You must know that.'

Laban knew it very well, but pretended to be surprised.

'My daughter! But my dear boy, my daughter is not a *wage*. She's an inheritance, a treasure, a wonder.'

'I won't ask for any wages at all. I'll work for you for nothing.'

'An inheritance, a treasure,' murmured Laban, looking closely into Jacob's eyes.

'I'll be your hired servant for no wages. I'd work for. . . for seven years for Rachel.' Jacob named an exaggerated period to show Laban just how much he really was in love. This would impress the older man. Jacob waited breathlessly. What would Laban suggest? A year? Six months?

'Very well,' said Laban at last. 'My daughter has to marry someone. She could do worse, I suppose, than marry you. Very well. Seven years it shall be.'

Seven years.

For the first time in his life, Jacob was speechless. He saw the pit which he had fallen into and it was of his own digging.

Before him lay a dreadful decision. Should he accept Laban's bargain and work without reward for seven years for Rachel, or walk 450 miles back home and be murdered by his jealous brother? To wander off in any other direction in romantic search for a fortune would, he knew, be madness.

He had little real choice. Jacob the swindler, Jacob the one who always comes out on top, had met his match. Laban had procured an heir for himself, someone who would carry on the family line from among his own people. And instead of paying this man who had dropped out of heaven into his lap a dowry, he was promised seven years' free labour. Laban stroked his beard and chuckled quietly.

Jacob snatched up a spade, tucked up his robe and began work on a new well. Seven years was not a lifetime. And it would be worth it for Rachel, oh Rachel. With his imagination for company Jacob dug many wells.

Weddings Haran-style

Jacob had attended weddings before, Esau had had several. But customs varied, even locally. Jacob was now to attend his own wedding and he was totally in the hands of his master, uncle and father-in-law-to-be.

It was certainly a lavish affair. No expense appeared to have been spared. Every inhabitant of the land from miles about was invited to a feast which lasted from dawn until well after nightfall.

The men and the women celebrated separately, of course, the symbolism emphasizing the dramatic coming together of the bride and groom at the end of the festivities. Jacob caught occasional glimpses of Rachel, always with her sister Leah. At a distance they looked very alike but their eyes were so different, Rachel's full of warmth and beauty and responsiveness, Leah's weak and empty, like looking into a pool with no water in it. Leah was older than Rachel but she was always distant and apparently passionless.

Early in the day Jacob thought that Laban was acting rather oddly, preoccupied it seemed, but the great feast was a heavy responsibility and Jacob could well understand his involvement.

As the day went on, Jacob found himself not really understanding anything very clearly. The wine flowed freely and the heat was oppressive. He remembered very little of the latter part of the evening. Faces came before him, smiling, congratulating him; Laban's face, close to his, smiling at him, or was he leering at him? Faces, faces everywhere, heat and torchlight and faces.

Then darkness, oh blessed darkness and quiet and the closeness of his beloved Rachel, clinging to him. After all these years, it was really true. If only he felt more aware of what was going on he could enjoy it properly. He sank again into a stupor.

Jacob became aware of light flooding the room. Consciousness returned. This was the room set aside for himself and Rachel. They had been married. His wife was in the bed beside him. He moved his eyes slowly, deliciously, over the ceiling and the wall, savouring the moment when he could wake his bride and look once more into those loving brown eyes. . . .

A thunderbolt would have shocked him less.

He found himself staring into a pool with no water in it – the weak, passionless eyes that he so disliked, but now pleading and full of fear.

It was Leah.

'My dear boy'

Jacob, predictably, stormed into Laban's quarters and demanded an audience. Laban was infuriatingly calm and friendly.

'But my dear boy, it's not our custom to marry the younger daughter before the elder. It wouldn't be right, you know. The elder carries the privileges. Esau was, or rather is, your elder brother, so you know all about that, don't you?'

That thrust cut deeply into Jacob's memory.

'But I worked seven years, *seven years*, for Rachel.'

'No, no. You worked seven years for my daughter. I never promised you Rachel by name.'

'But you knew that *I* meant Rachel!' Jacob was becoming more and more angry.

'My dear boy,' said Laban again, speaking more softly as Jacob's anger increased. 'Your interpretation of our agreement does not alter the wording of the agreement. I cannot possibly change the custom of our people. Didn't your father give you the Blessing of the Firstborn? You told me so. And he couldn't take it back. So with you and your marriage to Leah. It cannot be undone. Did you sleep with her?'

'Of course I did!'

'Well then.' Laban relaxed and sat back. 'But let's not be unreasonable. We are of the same family. I will tell you what we will do. Marry Rachel as well.'

'Oh, that's great! Two wives for the price of one!'

'No, there'll be a further arrangement.'

'*Further*! I suppose you're going to tell me to work for another seven years now!'

'Well now, I think that would be an excellent suggestion,' said Laban, smiling approvingly. 'You really do make the most helpful proposals. As a negotiator I find you to be very agreeable.'

By now Jacob's eyes were blazing. He glanced desperately round the room and Laban realized that he had gone too far. Jacob with a club in his hand would be a very determined negotiator indeed.

'But, look, Jacob, we must be reasonable. Let's make a bargain. It is the custom of our people that a husband and his new wife live together without any outside interference for a week. That's the honeymoon period. That we must insist upon. But then, after a week, let

Rachel come to you and be your wife as well. You will have two wives, with the chance to have twice as many children!'

Jacob's anger slipped away as the prospect of Rachel's love once more took hold of him. After this dreadful week he could leave Leah aside. She had a handmaid who could look after her. In the end, he would really be no worse off than before, except that his pride had had another knock and it would take a long time to recover from the shock of looking into those waterless eyes.

'Very well,' said Jacob at last, standing up and preparing to leave. 'Let it be as you say, and the Lord watch between us that we keep our bargains.'

'Indeed, indeed, well said, my boy, well said.' Laban bowed low and obsequiously and put his hands together in deference to their agreement and to the Lord who had been invoked.

Jacob thought, at that moment, how much he hated this slimy, scheming man who seemed able to outsmart anyone who crossed his path. He turned to go. As he reached the door, the honeyed tones came again.

'Oh, and Jacob. Another seven years I think we said, wasn't it? Yes, seven years I think.'

Jacob turned on his heel and strode away.

- ■ This story is told in Genesis chapter 29.
- ■ In what way was God honouring his promise to Jacob (Genesis 28:13–15)? Or had God abandoned him?
- ■ Does this dramatic story ring any bells with you (even if they are less dramatic)?

10

Sex, marriage and careers: Canwell Park

'I think it's your fault, Margaret.'

'*My* fault?' Margaret sounded exaggeratedly innocent.

'Yes, you invited me to supper with Nigel and Sallie and Bob so that Bob wouldn't feel left out. I know your devious mind, Margaret Barber. You were trying to get Bob and me together.'

'Well. . .' Margaret hesitated.

'All right, say no more, but now you've got us into this situation, how do you propose to get us out of it?'

'What situation exactly?'

'Of being front page news in the invisible *St Barnabas' Chronicle*. Mrs Goodrich saw us coming home late. Within twelve hours "The Haven" was buzzing like a hive. And now everyone at church sees us as romantically linked.'

'But you have been sitting together in church and walking together in the park. . .'

'Oh, so your spies have been out too!'

'Well, Shelley's bedroom looks out on the park.'

'And Shelley borrows Gordon's binoculars, I expect.'

'Gina!'

'I'm sorry, but can't you see we're being pushed by the dreaded gossip machine again?'

'But don't you like Bob?'

'Yes, I like him a lot. He's a dear. But we're not lovebirds.'

'I think Bob is.'

'That's one of the problems. Poor Bob. I don't think he's ever had a girlfriend in his life. Fifty-two and never been kissed. He's a very confirmed bachelor. And he's suddenly got bowled over.'

'And you, Gina, are the maiden who has bowled him.'

'I'm not a maiden, I'm a middle-aged widow.'

'So you don't think it could work?'

'Oh, *I* don't know.' Gina looked helplessly out of the window for inspiration and found none. 'He's a dear, yes, and very thoughtful. And he's a Christian, deep down in a quiet way. But I can't help remembering that he was on the side of the reactionaries who were against the change in the church furniture.'

'So was I.'

'Yes, I suppose so. But he's not very, well, *lively*, is he? And he's clever in his own technical area but he doesn't read books or go to the theatre or concerts. He's *dull*.'

'So you don't love him.'

Gina thought carefully. 'No, I don't,' she said, 'but if there weren't so many obstacles in the way, I suppose I might come to in time.'

'Poor Bob,' said Margaret. 'He's eating his heart out.'

'Well, as I said before, I think it's your fault, Margaret.'

The 'piece of paper'

The third in the series of marriage preparation classes was drawing to a close. The first two had been fairly uneventful. They had discussed the importance of communication, with which Nigel and Sallie quietly agreed, and the importance of spiritual closeness and praying together (with which Nigel and Sallie quietly disagreed), but the third session was about sexual relationships and had been very lively. Far from fainting if sex was mentioned, as Nigel had forecast, the members of the group became quite frank and uninhibited.

Somehow or other the subject of sex before marriage came up. Timothy, leading the discussion, tried to draw the fire away from Nigel and Sallie (in any case no-one wanted to attack them personally), but Nigel became defiant and defensive again, maintaining that Sallie and he were totally faithful to one another, had the liveliest intentions of getting married in a few months' time, and were, to all intents and purposes, married already. All that was needed was the 'piece of paper' which ratified the situation.

'And the blessing of the church,' added Timothy.

'Whatever that means,' said Nigel. Sallie screwed up her handkerchief and almost prayed that he wouldn't upset these people.

'I mean, you can't weigh or measure a blessing, can you? In what way are you better off with one than without? These children get a blessing every Sunday morning but they're no better than any other children. And since you're so hot on backing everything up from the Bible, where does it say in the Bible that you can't live together till after the wedding?'

'It's taken for granted, like the existence of God,' said Timothy. 'Young people weren't free to get together in those days as they are today. So they didn't have to be told not to.'

'Bet they did, though,' said Nigel.

'Nigel!' said Sallie.

'If you want some details,' Diana had a notebook on her knee, 'Deuteronomy 22:13–21 shows that a woman was expected to be a virgin when she married. And after Jacob had lived and worked for seven years in Laban's family, he said, "Give me my wife. . .I want to lie with her." That's a clear case after *seven years*! That's in Genesis 29:21.'

'And there's another example,' said Timothy. 'What about Joseph and Mary? She was still a virgin, although they were "betrothed" (which means something more definite than our engagement), and they didn't come together until after the child was born.'

'But they were special people, weren't they? You can't make a law from a single precedent like that.'

And so the debate had gone on. It ended amicably around the coffee cups but Sallie could feel that Nigel had been thoroughly wound up. They would need to continue with the subject later, or there would be no sleep for either of them.

'I almost wish we'd waited'

'What got into you, darling?' Sallie perched provocatively on the arm of Nigel's chair and smoothed back a stray lock of his hair. 'We said we wouldn't get into an argument with that group.'

'I've blown it, I suppose,' said Nigel morosely.

'There was no need to say anything. Now you've antagonized them.'

'That's the wrong word. They seem quite friendly still, you know. They accept us as we are.' There was a pause. 'It doesn't seem to worry them.'

'There's no reason why it should,' said Sallie. 'You said that yourself. And it certainly doesn't worry me. So who does it worry? It worries you, deep down, doesn't it, Nigel?'

Nigel stared at the French impressionist painting on the opposite wall.

'There just might be something in what they say.'

'Oh, Nige!'

'Timothy's probably right about the Bible, you know, sex is for marriage only and you remember what Diana said about unwrapping Christmas presents before Christmas Day? It leaves a bad taste. I almost wish. . .'

'Yes?'

'I almost wish we'd waited.'

'But, darling, you were arguing a few weeks ago that we shouldn't get married at all. Everything was so lovely. And now it's all spoilt. You, you don't love me any more, do you?' Sallie's lips quivered. Nigel put a reassuring arm round her waist.

'Of course I do. But don't you see what's happened? If we'd gone on living together without getting married we'd have been free from all these problems.'

'Exactly.'

'But we would also have been free from each other.'

'What do you mean?'

'We'd have been free to end it all if we felt like it. If you got a sudden passion for Bob Renshaw. . .'

'Or if you got turned on by Gina Holwell. . .'

'Quite. But because the marriage business ties us together much more definitely, anything that spoils it is the more damaging.'

'Well,' said Sallie, 'we can't undo what we've done. So let's make the best of it. Are you coming to bed?' She took his hand and pressed it against her cheek.

'OK,' said Nigel wearily.

But an hour and a half later Nigel was asleep in his chair. He awoke with a jerk to find Sallie bending over him in her nightdress. There were tears in her eyes.

Cameron Hogwood

Nigel sat on the underground train as he did every morning and watched with unseeing eyes as the names of the stations passed the windows: Fulham Broadway, West Brompton, Earl's Court. . .

Outwardly he appeared as he always did, immaculate in pin-stripe suit, carrying a black leather brief-case and a rolled umbrella. Not a hair was out of place. But inside his head there was turmoil.

What was the point of this church business? At the

office, of course, it had become known. His boss was not only taking every opportunity to make cutting remarks, just as Nigel had expected, but he was seriously having doubts about Nigel's fitness for the job. If he was going to develop a tender conscience towards the clients, the thrust might well go out of Nigel's work. Worse still, if things started to go wrong and Nigel was on the side of the angels, how could he be relied on to keep quiet? The prospect of Nigel testifying against him in court did not please Cameron Hogwood.

Nigel walked slowly up the steps and past the brightly gleaming plate that announced to the world that Crieff-Farbsteen was as solid gold an investment as you could hope to find in the Square Mile of the City of London. He usually ran up the steps. The uniformed commissionaire said, 'Good morning, sir,' as he always did, but Nigel didn't hear him.

His mind was with Sallie. It was the church again. The church had come between them and their heaven on earth. The church was ruining his career and ruining the best relationship he had ever had. No wonder he saw no uniform, no marble pillars, no mahogany reception desk. He didn't even see Janice in her crisp white blouse or hear her asking him why he looked like sour milk. The lift doors opened and there was Cameron Hogwood. He *would* be. This morning of all mornings.

'Morning, Saint Nigel.'

'Good morning, Cameron,' said Nigel with exaggerated precision.

'Now look here, Nigel, old feller.' Cameron put his arm round the younger man's shoulders. Nigel wished he wouldn't. 'No harm done, yer know. Just a bit of banter. But take my advice and keep your mind on your work. Work first. Family matters and religion are private affairs and no concern of mine. But Crief-Farbsteen *matters*. Get it?'

Nigel got it.

- Do you think it matters whether couples live together before marriage?
- Why?/why not?
- Is there anything in the 'Christmas present' argument?

11

Sex, marriage and careers: Haran

After seven years together in Haran honours were about even between Jacob and Laban. The old schemer had tricked Jacob twice, thus gaining cheap labour from a gifted herdsman for fourteen years (Jacob soon developed remarkable skills as a sheep-breeder), and disposed of his two daughters to his own kith and kin without paying a shekel of dowry. No wonder Laban was pleased with himself.

And Jacob? He had his heart's desire. Rachel, lovely Rachel, was his for ever. He had had to pay a terrible price for his bride, but it was worth it. Honours were about even.

So began, inauspiciously, the married life of Jacob, son of Isaac. He won an early concession from his father-in-law by demanding a regular wage. How could he keep

94

these young ladies in the manner to which they were accustomed if he was a mere slave? Laban saw the wisdom of that argument, but once more profited by the arrangement whereby he paid Jacob in sheep, rather than money. Any sheep Laban did not need or which were substandard he graciously consigned to the flock of Jacob. There was no fixed allowance. Jacob was later to complain that Laban had changed his wages ten times, so the changes were obviously not all in an upward direction.

'Give me children'

While Jacob was locked in an almost perpetual battle of wits with Laban, another conflict was being fought out in the women's quarters: Rachel versus Leah. In a household consisting of a wife who was hated, another who was adored and a couple of young handmaids there was bound to be trouble.

Genesis 29:31 observes that the Lord took a hand to redress the balance, so what Leah lacked in good looks and the love of her husband, she made up for by producing four healthy sons in rapid succession.

Rachel had no children. This was not through lack of effort on Jacob's part, we may be sure, but Rachel became increasingly bitter about the whole business. Jacob had sustained himself for seven years on the vision of brown eyes and his imagination of what it would be like when he had Rachel to himself. Now he discovered, as many have discovered before and since, that marriages cannot live by brown eyes and a vivid imagination alone.

Rachel blamed Jacob foursquare for her infertility (choosing to ignore the fact that Leah had had four sons by him).

95

'Give me children,' she demanded one memorable day, as if her husband had merely to walk to Haran market and buy a bundle of them. 'Give me children, or I shall die!' Whether this was a threat of suicide or fear of the mortification of the shame of childlessness is hard to say. Today we might call it a histrionic cry for attention. It attracted Jacob's attention all right, but not quite the kind she had expected. He rounded on her in fury, the fury aroused by someone who tries to blame someone else for her own failings.

'Give me children! Give me children! Who do you think I am, God almighty? What else do you think I can do about it, wave a magic wand?'

Rachel knew that she could gain nothing by using power tactics, so she fell back on an old custom.

'Take Bilhah, my maid. Have children by her. Then my shame will be reduced.' Had not Sarah herself suggested such a course to grandfather Abraham?

It worked. Bilhah produced a son and then another. Rachel was cock-a-hoop. 'I have had a struggle with my sister and I have won.'

Actually the score was four-two to Leah and Rachel could hardly claim the two as hers. But now Leah found *she* could have no more children. Not confident that a four-two lead was really enough to win in the end, she followed her sister's policy and gave Jacob *her* maid, Zilpah. Two more sons. Six-two. First set to Leah.

The pace hotted up. Leah's eldest, Reuben, found some mandrakes and brought them home as a present for his mum. Now mandrakes were prized aphrodisiacs (a word Reuben was yet to learn), and Rachel fixed her brown and beady eyes on them and demanded them for herself. Taking a calculated risk on the properties of the plants she said, 'Jacob can sleep with you tonight, if you give me the mandrakes.'

To Rachel's chagrin it went wrong. Leah produced two more sons and left Rachel holding the mandrakes. Eight-two and Leah had borne six of the eight herself. Then she had a daughter, Dinah.

Then, at last, when all seemed lost, Rachel became pregnant and Joseph was born. Years later the catalogue of family tragedies came to a climax when Rachel died giving birth to Benjamin.

Ten and two, twelve sons. So came into the world the founders of the twelve tribes of Israel, from a human point of view the issue of a sordid family mess. This story and the account of what happened next can be found, unvarnished, in Genesis 29 and 30. Unvarnished human passions, yet God had a plan for the family, and he had not given up on Jacob either.

An unpleasant siesta

It was siesta time, mid-afternoon on a hot summer's day. Laban was sitting in the shade, thinking sleepily about all that had happened to him in the past twenty years. Twenty years! His oldest grandchild would soon be thirteen, old enough to be considered a man. A good, strong lad, Reuben. He hadn't seen him lately. In fact he hadn't seen any of the family for several days. This was not unusual because the flocks were so huge now that they had to live apart for much of the time, to find pasture.

The triumph of those early years had worn rather thin. Jacob certainly had worked hard and had shown great skill as a manager of the flocks. Whether by cunning, superstition, good luck, prayer, or all four, Jacob's animals had increased vastly. He was a very rich man and Laban had often thought recently that it would be a good idea if they separated. There really wasn't room for both of them, and Jacob had an uncanny knack of succeeding in everything he attempted, despite the cruel tricks that Laban had worked on him. Strange. It was almost as if Jacob's god was looking after him.

Laban paid lip-service to Jacob's god (even using a capital G when Jacob was around) but Laban placed more reliance on his own household gods than on Elohim. The notion of a creator, God of the heavens, was too vast. He liked his gods where he could rely on them, over in the corner behind the curtain. On impulse he got up and drew back the curtain. The space was empty.

Who could have stolen them? He was not naïve enough to suppose that his gods were self-propelled. This was a serious matter. He called for his steward.

'Look at this! Who could have done this?'

The steward looked troubled. 'I do not know, but I have to tell you that Jacob saddled his camels and took all his flocks and belongings and his family and crossed the Euphrates with them.'

'When?'

'Three days ago.'

'Why didn't you tell me, you idiot? Quick! Check the flocks and the whole establishment. See what else they've stolen. The traitor! The black-hearted traitor!'

'May God watch us both'

And so it was that Laban took a small selection of his

household and close relatives as witnesses and pursued his son-in-law. It did not take him long to come up with the huge, lumbering mobile sheep-farm that was Jacob's stock-in-trade. He pitched his tents opposite Jacob's and waited for morning. In the night he dreamed that God, Jacob's God, was warning him not to harm Jacob. Dreams could be very inconvenient.

Their meeting was frosty. Laban's Hebrew eloquence set the tone of confrontation. In a querulous, high-pitched voice he began:

'Jacob, my dear boy, what have you done to me? What kind of gratitude do you call this? You have deceived your poor old uncle. You've stolen my daughters. If you had to go, why didn't you tell me in advance and we could have had a party, tambourines and harps? You didn't even let me kiss my grandchildren goodbye. My poor dear grandchildren' (he paused to wipe away a tear or two that were threatening to run down his beard).

'And now you have deserted me. Even your God is on your side. He came to me in a dream last night and told me not to punish you for this criminal act.'

'Laban, I have stolen nothing. Your daughters are *my* wives, remember? I worked fourteen years for them. These flocks are my flocks. I have worked six years for them. Is it my fault if God has increased my flocks and not yours? What crime have I committed?'

'You stole my gods.'

'Your *gods*! I did no such thing. You can search my whole encampment with pleasure and if anyone is found with your gods they shall die.'

Jacob was unaware that Rachel, his Rachel, was sitting in her tent, within earshot of this conversation, sitting on a saddle bag containing – Laban's idols.

Laban and his men searched thoroughly and found nothing. At last they came to the door of the women's tent.

'You don't suspect even your own daughters, do you?' Jacob was enjoying Laban's discomfiture.

'I trust nobody,' said Laban, and defying all courtesies, marched into the tent. Rachel sat still and eyed her father.

'Excuse my not rising,' she said in honeyed tones, 'but', and her voice sank to a confidential whisper, 'it is the wrong time of the month for me.' She looked coolly at him. His gaze, full of suspicion, held hers for a moment then wavered. He strode into the sunshine.

'Jacob! You'll pay for this. You've stolen my gods and I don't know what you've done with them. My daughters, maidservants, grandchildren, flocks, everything. Everything you can see here is mine. You're a thief, Jacob, a thief!'

Jacob knew that he held the initiative now and could afford to be conciliatory.

'Look, Laban, God appeared to you last night. We'll make a solemn agreement, in God's name, that I will stay beyond this place and never come back to trouble you again.'

'Very well, Jacob. And may God watch us both that we keep our vows. If you stay that side of this place and protect my daughters and take no other wives, then I will not harm you.'

So they gathered stones, set up a monument, a cairn of witness, and parted, never to meet again, each calling upon God to avenge him on the other. They ate a solemn meal together, then Laban kissed his daughters and his grandchildren and returned to Haran with a heavy heart.

Meanwhile, back in Canwell Park

Sallie, as usual, arrived home first. She pushed open the front door and gathered up the heap of junk mail, bills and catalogues that always seemed to drift against it like driven snow.

She followed her usual custom of taking a shower as soon as she got in, 'washing London out of her hair' as she put it, rolled herself in a huge, warm towel which she then exchanged for a soft dressing gown, and sat down to open the post.

To her astonishment there was an envelope without a stamp on it, addressed 'My darling' in Nigel's handwriting. It wasn't an anniversary or a birthday. She stared at the envelope, hardly daring to open it. Something was wrong. It must be.

It was.

She found it difficult to believe it, but Nigel was telling her that he was moving out. For a trial period. He assured her that this would not affect plans for the wedding. They could continue to go to the marriage preparation classes. And the church. But it would be much better for all concerned if he moved in to his aunt's flat in Kensington (she was hardly ever there). They could go on paying the mortgage jointly as before but they would be able to 'sort themselves out' before the wedding.

Sallie screwed up the letter and flung herself on to the hearthrug in a fit of uncontrolled sobbing. They didn't need to sort themselves out. They'd been fine before this church business started. Who did God think he was, bursting in and interfering with their lovely relationship?

Even in the passion of the moment Sallie remembered that she didn't believe in God, at least not in a God who interfered with anything.

And Nigel! Hard-headed Nigel! He was never moved by people smiling at one another. Everything was measured by profit and loss for Nigel. This was totally out of character. How could they get married if he'd walked out on her like this? He might do it again. What sort of preparation was it for being together to live apart? And how could they go together to church as if nothing had happened? They'd be living a lie. The irony of this thought escaped Sallie in her distress.

She remembered Nigel again. He was her life. Nigel, darling. And he needed her. How could he look after himself? His aunt was never there. But could it be? It *might* be. Janice, the girl on reception. She was always very friendly with Nigel. He joked about it. That was it. Nigel's loss might be his home and Sallie, but his profit was Janice. . .

Sallie experienced a darkness deeper than she had ever imagined possible. Wave after wave of bitterness swept over her. She was still lying on the floor when her neighbour, fearing the worst, rushed in to find out why she had not answered the telephone.

- Two stories of people separating for their own good.
- Is it true that people who really love each other should be together all the time?
- Or is a bit of distance a good idea sometimes?

12

More appointments with God

The City of London is a unique monument to human endeavour. The City, that is, the Square Mile, is bounded by the Tower of London and the Thames to the south and the remains, or the course, of the medieval city wall round about.

The City is crammed with temples, shrines to the goddesses of profit, capital, interest and investment. They soar into the air like giant fingers reaching out to the heavens for higher returns. Brokers, bankers, agents, conveyancers, financiers of every kind work long and frantic hours, keeping a moment-by-moment watch on computer screens which reflect the current state of affairs in the stock-markets of Paris, Frankfurt, Tokyo and New York.

On closer examination these towers erected to the glory of man are seen to be not alone. Peeping out between them, dwarfed and apparently buried by them, can be seen churches, seemingly tiny and insignificant yet bravely pointing to the clear sky above them. The bulk of St Paul's Cathedral alone competes with its secular rivals in size, but many are the places of worship where the God of love and sacrifice is honoured among the temples of high finance.

Before the Great Fire destroyed most of them in 1666 there were churches on almost every street corner in London. Sir Christopher Wren and his contemporaries made good the damage as best they could, but their white and glistening wedding cakes and campaniles stand now grey and apparently lifeless, diminished by bombing, tombstones to a lost civilization, suffered to remain as sepulchres to the dead.

'Wolfy's Up-the-Wall'

One of these grey stone monuments sat uneasily next door to the London headquarters of Crieff-Farbsteen. It was called St Wulfstan's. In fact its full name was St Wulfstan-on-the-Wall with St Eggburga Without, but it was generally and rather unkindly known as 'Wolfy's Up-the-Wall'. Its lifeless appearance and its unfortunate nickname gave the visitor a foreboding of spiders, bats and at best a cup of weak tea and a few pious platitudes from a crazy cleric.

Little could have been further from the truth, for twice a week, in the lunch break, the church was packed to overflowing with City workers. Thick red carpets and bright lights were the background to short but vibrant addresses which applied biblical principles to modern life, even life in the City.

About half-way back and at the end of the row, sheltering behind a pillar, were two identically dressed young men. One sat back with his arms folded, delighted to have persuaded his friend to come with him at last. The other sat with hunched shoulders, and peered gloomily at the closed hymn book on the shelf in front of him. Nigel was not listening to the speaker. He was, predictably, thinking about Sallie. He found it difficult to think about anything else. She had told him in no uncertain terms what she thought of his 'walking out on her', and although he had been able to talk to her and make her see his point of view, she was still very unhappy and insecure. Nigel asked himself for the hundred and tenth time whether he was doing the right thing. The trouble now was that he couldn't easily climb down and return to Sallie. It had become a matter of principle and he was a stubborn man.

The speaker had been making a comparison between the City, as understood by contemporary social commentators, and the City of God as described in the Bible. He was nearing the end of his talk and, for some reason, snippets of what he had to say began to filter into Nigel's conscious mind.

The speaker was reading now from Revelation, the description of John's vision of the perfect city:

> *I saw the Holy City, the new Jerusalem, coming down out of heaven from God, prepared as a bride beautifully dressed for her husband. And I heard a loud voice from the throne saying, 'Now the dwelling of God*

is with men, and he will live with them.
They will be his people, and God himself
will be with them and be their God. He will
wipe away every tear from their eyes. . .'
(Revelation 21:2–4).

A city coming down from heaven

If only this whole muddle of himself and Sallie and the church and the business could all be swept away and they could start again. The 'new Jerusalem'. Something awoke in Nigel's imagination. New.

The reader was continuing, 'He who was seated on the throne said, "I am making everything new!"'

That would be wonderful if it were not all pie in the sky. Sallie had said that. Tears came to Nigel's eyes and he blew his nose loudly and buried his face in his handkerchief. But hadn't he just heard, 'He will wipe away every tear from their eyes'? Anyway, God, if there really is a God, is far away up in heaven. He couldn't have any real relevance.

. . . 'He who overcomes will inherit all this, and I will be his God and he will be my son.'

This was astonishing. Every question that came to his mind was apparently answered by the next verse the speaker read. He'd finished now and was saying a prayer, but Nigel's mind was still busy with this new dimension that had suddenly opened before him.

Of course it wasn't real. It was all picture language. But the thought struck him with such force that it was as if someone had heard his thought and spoken aloud:

'Yes, it is picture language, but the reality behind it is greater than the picture.'

106

A city coming down from heaven? That was an impossible picture. You couldn't imagine it. What was the reality behind that? 'The dwelling of God is with men, and he will live with them.'

So true religion was not people posturing and pretending and trying to find God, as Nigel had always supposed. True religion was *God* coming down to live with human beings. Just when he was needed. To make everything new again. To wipe away tears. . .

Nigel buried his face in his hands again. In his present state of distress the way that reading fitted together and seemed to apply to him personally was something he had never experienced before. He had a sudden remembrance of the worshippers at Canwell Park smiling at one another, something that had so impressed Sallie. Suddenly he understood what they had to smile about.

Four hundred men

Jacob, however, was not smiling. His great caravan had slowly wound its way across the empty wastelands, a long zig-zag journey as he moved from one area of grassland to another, limited always by the need to feed his enormous flocks.

He had had news of Esau, now living far to the east of their original home, across the Jordan in Edom. Messages had been exchanged. Jacob had swallowed hard and had sent a messenger, instructed to say: 'A request from his servant Jacob to my master Esau. I have been staying with Laban our uncle all these years. I have cattle and donkeys, sheep and goats, menservants and maidservants. I am sending this message so that I might ask for peace.'

The bit about the servant to the master ought to go down well. No point in mentioning wives and children at this stage. It would only remind Esau that he, Esau, had married into the wrong circles and perhaps provoke him to hostility.

The messengers were gone for several days and Jacob waited impatiently. At last they returned, but with no joy in their faces.

'What did he say?' demanded Jacob.

'He said nothing.'

'Not a word?'

'Not a single word, but he is coming to meet you.'

'That's good. I'm glad to hear that.'

'He is coming with four hundred men.'

Jacob could not remember ever being more frightened. A black despair seemed to descend on him. His small band of servants could not possibly engage an army of four hundred. Even in despair, however, Jacob's wits did not leave him.

He quickly divided all his possessions into two sections, reasoning that if Esau's men attacked one, at least the other might escape. He also prepared wave after wave of gifts for Esau, flocks of choice goats, sheep, cattle, camels, each intended to soften the heart of his vengeful brother. It was just possible that the sheer, calculating generosity of Jacob's offerings might melt Esau. But when he had finished making all these arrangements the mood of despair descended on Jacob again and he sat down and buried his face in his hands.

And he prayed.

Yes, Jacob prayed. Not this time a bargaining with God such as he had made twenty years ago. Gone was the posturing, the assurance that he, Jacob, had a right to bandy words with God. In its place a fear, a fear not only for himself but for his wives and children; an honesty – he no longer pretended to be on top of the situation – and a humble reminder to God that it was he who had called Jacob to leave Haran and therefore had a duty to see him safely home.

So Jacob did not raise his hands to the sky nor did he so much as lift up his eyes to heaven, but prayed to his God as he sat with his head in his hands:

> 'O God of my father Abraham, God of my father Isaac, O LORD, who said to me, "Go back to your country and your relatives, and I will make you prosper," I am unworthy of all the kindness and faithfulness you have shown your servant. I had only my staff when I crossed this Jordan, but now I have become two groups. Save me, I pray, from the hand of my brother Esau, for I am afraid he will come and attack me, and also the mothers with their children. But you have said, "I will surely make you prosper and will make your descendants like the sand of the sea, which cannot be counted"'
> (Genesis 32:9–12).

Never before in his life had Jacob confessed to being afraid, never had he expressed his own unworthiness and never acknowledged God's kindness and faithfulness. And never had he felt such a surge of inner peace

109

as he did as he finished his prayer. God had put him in this situation and God was quite capable of taking charge. He would leave the outcome in God's hands.

He made final arrangements, seeing his wives and children safely across the ford of the River Jabbok and lay down to a deep and dreamless sleep such as he had not experienced, it seemed, for years.

- Try to give a totally fair and unbiased answer to these questions:
- Is my life so important to me that God stands outside it?
- Or is God so important to me that my life circles round him?
- Can I explain this difference to someone else?

13

Focus on Sallie

Sallie Peterson walked up Fairview Avenue, looking for number sixty-seven. Her jeans and her sweater fitted her as snugly as ever but the spring was absent from her step. Her hair looked just a little untidy and her shoulders slightly bowed. A close look at her eyes suggested sleeplessness and weeping, though the make-up disguised her problems from the casual passer-by.

She found the house she was looking for and rang the doorbell. She turned casually and thought she saw a curtain move in the house opposite. She was unaware of the existence of Mrs Goodrich.

Gina Holwell was at the door in a moment and Sallie found herself being embraced, no continental kiss now but a wordless welcome of genuine warmth. If anyone could help Sallie Gina could, though she feared that Gina might preach at her and tell her what a wonderful man Nigel was to have the courage of his convictions. But Gina seemed to be on her side at the moment.

Life in an empty house

Gina listened patiently while Sallie poured out her feelings of frustration and anger. The house was empty and lonely. It was too big. She had no friends locally. She felt that the church people were mocking her, treating her as a Jezebel, when she was probably more faithful to one man than many of the church members were. Gina winced.

Life was a sham. Here was Nigel, all care and loving attention, calling to take her to church, calling to go to the marriage preparation classes, taking her home again, drinking coffee with her, embracing her tenderly and, just when she needed him most, saying goodbye and leaving her alone for the night. Just to satisfy his conscience. It was too much!

There was a long silence while Sallie transferred some mascara to a tissue, thoughtfully provided by Gina.

'When's the wedding, Sallie?'

'Oh, I don't know. I can't see that there'll ever be a wedding.'

'Sallie, when is the wedding arranged for?'

'November, I think.'

'What day in November?'

'Oh, the twenty-first.'

'That's just over six months.'

'Exactly!' burst out Sallie again. 'I can't live for six whole months in an empty house!'

Gina looked steadily at Sallie and said nothing. Sallie became aware that Gina lived alone in a house more than big enough for two.

'It's not only the house, it's the frustration of having Nigel there and not there. We've had a wonderful sex life together. How can I survive for six months without it?'

Gina was silent again and Sallie remembered that Gina had been a widow for five years or more.

'I'm sorry, Gina. I suppose you've managed somehow. But I just can't imagine any two people enjoying such a love as we've had.'

'Perhaps we all think that,' said Gina quietly, 'but I can tell you quite certainly that it is possible to live without sex for five years. It's hard sometimes but the sun still shines, the rain still falls and all the other satisfactions of life are still there.'

'There aren't any other satisfactions,' said Sallie.

'Of course you can't feel that at the moment,' said Gina, 'but I am telling you for a fact that there are. And six months is a remarkably short time, you know. If I were in your position I'd be getting frantic about bridesmaids, lists of guests and my dress. Have you got your dress yet?'

Sallie looked up, and for the first time, Gina thought, appeared interested in something. She had touched a positive note. The thought of Sallie in a fabulous wedding gown and the breathtaking risk of asking Shelley Barber to be her bridesmaid took the conversation into more tranquil waters.

God's practical answer

Sallie returned home half an hour later with a slightly lighter heart than she had come with and a flick of the curtain at number sixty-four registered her departure.

Gina closed the door thoughtfully and returned to her chair. That had been a useful interview. Sallie really did seem to have taken on board some positive hope. Gina wondered whether she should have talked to Sallie about her need of the Lord, the ultimate answer to her need for satisfaction. On reflection it was perhaps better not. The practical ideas involved in preparing for the wedding had sent Sallie away with a bit of a spring in her step – a sermon, at this stage, would probably have crushed her. Gina nevertheless prayed again that both Sallie and Nigel would come to the Light of the World instead of grasping after success and a big bank balance.

Yes, the interview had been useful, but it had left Gina herself very uneasy. Why? Was her conscience still troubling her that she hadn't talked about God, or prayed with Sallie? No, she was sure she had done the right thing there. Had she talked too much and not listened sympathetically enough? No, she'd managed not to make comparisons between Sallie and herself. Sallie had seen the point without Gina's promptings.

The real problem was that Sallie's expressing her deep feelings about Nigel had awakened Gina's own. About Andrew. She had not allowed herself to remember Andrew. The pain would have been too great. But now, this vivacious young bride-to-be had broken the barrier so carefully erected and Gina gave herself up to a rush of memories about herself and Andrew.

'I just can't imagine any two people enjoying such a love as we've had.' Sallie's words were repeating themselves. Little could Sallie know! She was young and inexperienced, however worldly-wise she appeared on the surface.

Gina, despite her best intentions, surrendered to her imagination and her memories of Andrew. . .

The 'phone bell sliced through her dreams and forced her abruptly back to the present.

'Oh, hello, Bob, how nice to hear you!'

Bob! What a contrast! What a come-down! From a motel on the road to heaven to a flat in Basingstock Road, in five seconds.

'Yes, of course I'd like to come. . .OK, seven-thirty. See you, Bob.'

Dear old Bob. He saw Gina as a friend, not a lover. He explained the intricacies of the Underground system to her as a small boy delights in his model railway. But he was alive and he admired her. And Andrew would never return. Perhaps Bob was God's practical answer to her loneliness just as wedding preparations were for Sallie's. 'The rain still falls, and all the other satisfactions of life are still there.'

Who had said that?

'Nigel's gone mad'

'Now, what's all this about, Gordon?'

Although they worked for the same firm, Gordon had never asked Sallie to have lunch with him before, and even now he was wondering whether he would tell Margaret and whether she would start getting suspicious.

'Oh yes, there is something. You know about the St Barnabas' church development fund, don't you? I've had a letter from Nigel about it. Did he tell you what was on his mind?'

'Not a word,' said Sallie.

'He's thinking of making a fairly substantial donation, a matter of thousands.' There was a pause.

'Nigel's gone mad.'

'Well, we have to look at this from several angles. Nigel's insanity was not one I had in mind. But why do you think he's doing it?'

'If I know Nigel, which I think I do, and if he's not gone mad, which I hope he hasn't, I should say he was investing the money for some kind of return. He wants to buy a stake in the good offices of the church. To be somebody – have a seat on the board – you know the kind of thing?'

'But you can't buy a seat on the board of a parish church.'

'No, but you can become known as a benefactor. "Look, there goes good old Nigel. A big church giver, you know."'

'You sound rather bitter.'

'Yes, I am. We can do with all the thousands we can lay hands on at the moment. Weddings are not cheap. Neither are mortgages. I shall have some words with him.'

'Well, don't be too hard on him,' said Gordon. 'I get the impression that he has a genuine desire to express his gratitude to the church. In his letter he talks about his eyes being opened to true values and how short-sighted we are to worship money in today's society.'

'It's what I said then. Nigel's gone mad.'

'There's another difficulty, you know.'

'Which is?'

'I don't know whether the church ought to accept the money.'

'But you need a third of a million! A few thou. would go down well.'

'Yes, but ought the church to accept money that has indirectly come from old-age pensioners who have invested their life savings in doubtful share issues? You see what I mean?'

'I think I see, but I don't agree. From your point of view you shouldn't ask where the money's been. Just be grateful for where it's going. But whatever has made Nigel want to do this? And why didn't he tell me first? Do you think it's conscience-money? A way to pay for his behaviour to me?'

'I think his conscience is clearer now than it has been for years, if you want my opinion.'

'Is it, though?' Sallie looked thoughtful. 'Helen said she'd seen him in Town with Janice again. I don't think his conscience is in credit somehow.'

'Helen is the worst gossip-monger I have ever met,' said Gordon vehemently, pausing with his spoon poised over his chocolate gateau. He looked hard at Sallie.

'Do you really believe he's having an affair with this Janice? Do you really trust him as little as that?'

Sallie reddened.

'I suppose I've got a suspicious mind,' she said. 'I've been pretty fed up myself these past weeks. It wouldn't take much to get me into bed with a healthy young guy. Why should Nigel be any different? Oh dear! Now I've shocked you. I'm so sorry, Gordon. Forget what I said.'

'No, no, it's all right,' mumbled Gordon, 'I can sympathize with you, I do assure you. But I think you can trust Nigel.'

Sallie leaned over and kissed him.

Gordon wondered guiltily what Margaret would have thought about that.

- What gives you most real satisfaction?
- If that is removed, have you anything else to fall back on?
- What kind of satisfaction can God offer to you?

14

The Great Contest: Jacob

It was odd, thought Timothy, how crises seemed to come simultaneously. Obviously in a church there will always be some people in trouble every week. It was as statistically likely as someone having a birthday, but at the moment there seemed to be so many serious problems that a sense of impending doom hung in the air, like the approach of a thunderstorm on a sultry day in summer.

The church's major concern was the appeal fund for the new building. Many weary meetings had been held and long debates about the relative merits of sending money to the Third World and spending it on themselves. Sacrificial giving had taken place but their target figure still seemed far over the horizon. Timothy winced as he thought yet again of the good people on both sides of the debate and wondered how you distinguished faith from folly. They were all responsible and understanding people but the buck, whatever that was, rested on Timothy's desk. People were obediently writing large cheques, and it was his responsibility.

Then there were Bob and Gina. They had both asked for his advice and he had gladly given it, but it didn't seem to solve their problem: should they go ahead or not?

Worse still, Sallie and Nigel seemed to be heading for a dramatic break-up. They were both headstrong and stubborn. Timothy admired Nigel's move and believed it had been the right one, but Sallie's attitude seemed to be hardening. Gordon was doing his best to hold them together, good old Gordon, but what hurt Timothy most was the fact that this situation had been caused by the church's biblical stance on pre-marital relationships. Certainly Nigel had acted on his own initiative. He had not been ordered by the church to move out. And certainly this standard was the right one and should not be relaxed. It was for the good of the couples too. But that didn't prevent Timothy from feeling deeply for them, especially as he compared their tumultuous relationship with his own with Diana and their excitement at the forthcoming addition to their family.

He sighed deeply and turned to his prayer. What a wonderful thing it was, he reflected, that he could share all these cares and worries with a loving God who understood them all and had experienced them himself in the person of Jesus. If there were to be disasters, he knew that God was with them in the disasters. He prayed earnestly for each of the people in turn. When he had finished he knew that he had done the right thing.

But the sense of impending disaster remained with him.

The storm breaks

Jacob had lain down to sleep in peace. Perhaps for the first time in his life he had prayed a sincere and humble prayer. He feared that Esau his brother was coming against him to wreak a terrible vengeance but he had made up his mind that God was in charge, so he had arranged his possessions as best he could.

In all this his old cunning had not deserted him. Dividing his flocks and herds was prudent, and sending forward gifts to placate Esau was a calculated act of policy. Now he had sent his family, his wives, maidservants and eleven sons across the river and remained by himself on the far bank. Like the fabled Duke of Plaza-Toro in Gilbert and Sullivan's *The Gondoliers*:

> *In exercise of martial kind, when there was*
> *   any fighting,*
> *He led his regiment from behind, he found*
> *   it less exciting.*

So Jacob lay down and slept contentedly. He had prayed, made all the arrangements he could, assured his own personal safety and was very well pleased with himself.

He awoke with a start. It was still dark, though there

was a luminosity in the eastern sky which suggested that the night was well advanced. There was no sound, no cause for alarm. Yet Jacob did feel alarmed, in fact deeply troubled. How could you go to sleep in such contentment and then wake a few hours later in a panic?

He told himself firmly that everything was fine. He went over his plans once again, ticking them off mentally and trying to assure himself that all was in order, but the sense of brooding calamity deepened. He stood up and looked about him. Nothing moved. Even the night creatures seemed to be holding their breath.

With no warning a violent blow flung Jacob to the ground and he found himself pinned down by an assailant who had apparently sprung out of the earth, so silently had he approached.

Jacob did not think. It was no time for deciding on priorities. He resisted. Automatically he counter-attacked, forced his opponent to give way and rounded on him. Words seemed out of place. What was the point of saying, 'Excuse me, I think you've got the wrong man', or 'You won't find any money here'?

Both men were wiry and tough and not in-experienced in the art of self-defence. As Jacob reflected on the incident later he remembered that the thought had flashed through his mind that Esau had found him out, but he would have recognized Esau. It also came to him that he had made a big mistake in staying alone on the north side of the ford, but it was too late now. The logical thing to do would have been to ask this man who he was and what he wanted and suggest they talk about it, but when you are bowled over suddenly in the middle of a peaceful night you are not always logical. One thought only was uppermost in Jacob's mind now: 'Don't give in. . .hang on.'

So the two were locked in combat, crashing through the undergrowth, once falling into the shallows of the river, first one in the ascendant, then the other, pausing by mutual and silent consent occasionally to recover their breath and then back to it with renewed energy for what seemed like hours. The dawn began to break.

'Hang on'

As the contest continued Jacob began to realize that this was no ordinary desert thief or wandering tribesman. For some reason he did not seem to be anxious to finish the fight. He was not murderous. He seemed to be almost leading Jacob on to test his stamina. And Jacob found his resolve stiffening with every minute. 'I must hang on.' His stubbornness and determination were stretched to the limit but still he hung on.

Then suddenly a violent pain shot through Jacob's hip. The odd thing was that he had not fallen on it or twisted it. The stranger had merely touched it and it felt as if it had been dislocated. In his pain and agony Jacob held on even more desperately.

At last the silence was broken.

'Let me go now,' said the stranger. 'The day is breaking.'

Whether Jacob sensed that this man had some supernatural power, whether he wanted his assurance that he would not attack again or whether his innate bargaining power grasped at the chance to make something out of the deal, Jacob heard himself saying,

'I will not let you go unless you give me a blessing.'

'What is your name?' came the response.

Now to divulge one's name in that culture was to be open with a very precious thing, surrendering one's identity and sharing one's very self. But for some reason Jacob trusted this mysterious stranger. Even as he spoke his own name he remembered its meaning: 'heel grasper', 'swindler', 'cheat'.

'Your name shall be no more "heel grasper", but Israel. You have struggled with God and with men and you have succeeded.'

'What is your name, then?' asked Jacob at last. 'Who are you?'

'Why do you ask?' said the stranger. 'Receive the blessing and be content. For you are Israel, the father of many peoples, and you have found favour with God.'

Jacob raised his eyes to respond to the stranger and he was just not there.

From sheer exhaustion and pain Jacob collapsed where he was and fell into a dazed sleep.

The face of God

The sun was up when he awoke again. Another dream then! At important stages of his life Jacob seemed to be the recipient of dreams, fantastic, violent dreams, presumably meant to teach him something.

He remembered this one very clearly as he lay motionless on the ground beside the river. What did it mean?

One obvious interpretation would be that he had met

an angel in his dream, a messenger of God. He had brought a blessing, a message to say that all was going to be well. But whatever was all that wrestling for? It seemed an odd way to deliver a message.

Then Jacob remembered the words, 'You have struggled with God.' Perhaps the stranger represented God himself. Yes, that was it, Jacob had spent his whole life struggling with other people but this dream episode was sent to show him that he had been struggling against God as well. The idea swept over him with intense clarity. Struggling with God! He had made bargains with God and tried to use God. He had never submitted to God or volunteered to serve him.

But why should God, if it were he, ask Jacob to let him go? It was clear again. He meant, 'Jacob, stop struggling with me. You can never win, you know. Let me go and let me be God to you. I will not force my way with you but I will let you know who is in charge.'

Then that touch on the hip had been a sign of what God could do if he wanted to. That had been excruciating. Jacob felt his hip gingerly. It seemed normal. He relaxed and considered his dream again. This new name, Israel, suggested that he had been in a contest with God and had won! Surely that couldn't be right. No, the touch on the hip had been a warning not to imagine himself on equal terms. The victory had been God's all the time. The victory was in Jacob's desire to be blessed. During that violent wrestling match Jacob's struggle against God, the attempt to keep him out of his life, had been transformed into a struggle to invite God into his life. 'Please stay out' had become 'Please come in.' It needed a vivid dream, thought Jacob, to teach me all that. Well, that was good, and now it was time to think about Esau.

Jacob propped himself up on his elbows, half rolled over and sprang to his feet.

Just as quickly he collapsed to the ground in an agony of pain. Something really had happened to his hip joint.

As he crawled painfully across to a thicket to trim for himself a stick to support his weight, it dawned on him in full measure that his dream had been no dream at all. It was all true. It had happened. He had seen God face to face and yet his life had been spared.

He struggled across the stream, limping heavily and bearing on his stick, and the light became ever stronger from the rising sun.

'I shall call this place Peniel, face of God,' he muttered as he looked back to the scene of the night's drama, 'and my life has been spared.'

El Elohe Israel

When you have met God face to face, meeting your brother is a relatively small matter. The episode of the wrestling is described in Genesis 32:22–32. Jacob's meeting with Esau occupies chapter 33.

It is enough to record that the meeting was a surprising one. 'Esau ran to meet Jacob and embraced him; he threw his arms around his neck and kissed him. And they wept' (33:4).

Jacob pressed Esau to accept his generous gifts, even though Esau had plenty for himself. Esau's warm-hearted but unwise proposal that they should go on together, Jacob characteristically evaded. It was clear that their new relationship could not survive if they

126

tried to feed their enormous flocks and herds on the same ground. In fact, Jacob promised to follow Esau but then went the other way. Well, nobody becomes perfect overnight. But there is no doubt that Jacob, now Israel, was a fundamentally changed man.

One remark that he let slip to Esau is evidence of it. 'To see your face is like seeing the face of God, now that you have received me favourably' (33:10). This was not mere flattery. Never before would Jacob have thought of God as one who received him favourably. He really had seen the face of God and knew what he was talking about.

When he settled near Shechem Jacob erected a memorial altar, and its name was *El Elohe Israel*, 'Mighty is the God of Israel'.

In the great contest, God had won. And therefore so had Israel.

- Is your life a constant struggle?
- Who are you struggling with:
    Yourself?
    Other People?
    God?

15

Building fund in crisis

T he steering committee was in session in the vicarage sitting room. The atmosphere was electric. The appeal fund had reached a critical stage. Of the £355,000 needed, £185,000 had been received or promised and a further £55,000 promised in interest -free loans.

The amount of money raised in such a short time by a relatively few people was astonishing, but they were still a long way from the target, £115,000 to be precise. Many people had given sacrificially and could hardly be expected to give yet more.

Cyril Kent was deeply disturbed by the whole affair and made sure the meeting was in no doubt about it.

'It's not simply a question of fund-raising and asking people to give as they are able,' he was saying. 'In a situation like this people's consciences are being manipulated. Good biblical teaching on responsible giving is one thing, but urging people to meet an enormous target like this is quite another.

'It's all right for thick-skinned people who can weigh up all the pros and cons and decide that they will give x pounds and that is all. But there are some sensitive people who have given a lot of their savings to this appeal. Who knows whether they will need the interest from those savings to live on? I know of several people who have sold valuable family antiques. People who are going without holidays that they badly need. A kind of giving-fever has been started, and it's hard to know where it might end. What I object to is the pressure, almost blackmail, to see this work through, a work which, as you know, I don't think is at all necessary in the first place.'

'Thank you, Cyril. . . ,' said Timothy, but before he could say anything further Fred Jenkins was in full flow.

'Feed the hungry'

'I've supported this idea all the way, as you know, Vicar, and I shall go on supporting it. It's not that we ask people to give too much. We ask them to give too little.

'God knows what he's doing and he has his funds available. All we have to do is respond in a biblical way. Jacob promised a tenth of all his income to God, didn't he? I've been doing some sums and I reckon that if everyone in this church gave a tenth of their income to the church we should have about a quarter of a million coming in every year. At that rate we could pay for this sort of improvement about every three or four years and still have enough for charities. The problem is that some people give a lot but most people find excuses not to give at all.'

129

This was too much for Connie Bassett. Connie had been appointed to the committee as the spokesperson for the 'commonsense senior citizen' as she put it.

'Fred Jenkins,' she said, 'don't talk to me about quarters of millions! How many people at this church is pensioners? Dozens of us! We don't work in the City with stockbrokers nor nothing. The church can 'ave two pounds ten shillings from me and it's lucky to get it, I say. So don't come your millions 'ere.'

'I don't think we need record in public how much each of us is giving,' said Timothy quickly, 'but I do agree with Fred that a team effort, everyone working together, will succeed where a few heroic individuals will fail. So we *do* appreciate your two pounds, er, fifty pence, Connie. We honour you for it and so, I'm sure, does the Lord himself. Remember the widow's mite.'

'What might the widows have done, then?' asked Connie innocently. At that stage of the meeting it was the best thing she could have said. Order was restored after a ten-minute break for coffee.

Then another much-debated objection was raised, this time by John Morrison, who represented the young people's action group. He held a piece of paper in his hand and was obviously embarrassed as the only person under twenty-five present, but he spoke with a determined voice.

'The YP have had a prayer meeting about this,' he began. 'Good for them', 'Well done!', 'Puts us to shame,' came encouraging responses from around the room.

'We don't know what the church should be doing but we believe that it's our job to feed the hungry. Ethiopia, Sudan, Mozambique and,' he paused, 'places like that, are much more needy than Canwell Park. We need a building to feel comfortable in. They need food even to live.

'So we have agreed to raise £1,000 in the next year, by sponsored swims, bike rides and a lot of other ways, to send to relief agencies who will provide food and water and Christian literature to Africa where it's needed. So I'm afraid we can't help the building fund.'

Several people clapped enthusiastically at this. Timothy looked at Gordon Barber.

'John, I think that's great,' said Gordon. 'It just could be that this appeal is awakening people to see the needs of a much wider world. Timothy and I have been working on this and want to propose that, whichever way the decision goes about the fund, as a church we should aim to double our giving to the Third World from the end of this year.

'But what we have to decide today is whether to call a halt to the development fund here (and if we do, we shall need to decide what to do with the money so far given or pledged) or whether to continue with it. The builders are moving in next Monday. We need £115,000 more. They expect to take about eight months, though I suspect it could be the best part of a year, and we shall need to pay them by the end of that time.

'A bank loan, if we could get one, would involve us in very heavy interest repayments. You have a sheet of figures so I don't need to say any more. How shall we proceed, Timothy?'

The vote

'I think we can agree to a decision taken on a majority vote,' said Timothy. 'There are ten of us and I as chairman shall abstain. So our first and major decision is whether to abandon the project in its present form, and if we do, we shall need to agree on some alternative.'

Gordon made a plea for faith, courage and determination to continue with the work, begun so well, and Timothy called for a few minutes of prayer before the decision was taken. Gordon was miserable. From what had been said it was clear that the vote would be about six or seven to three or two against proceeding. Had all that work been wasted? All those hopes to be extinguished?

The prayer ended, and Gina Holwell, who had been unusually silent, waved her hand.

'Yes, Gina,' said Timothy, grateful for further postponement of the vote.

'I would like to propose the motion in specific terms,' said Gina. 'If God wants us to proceed with this scheme, he will send us a sign. I suggest that we agree on a figure which we ask him to provide by the end of the week. If that money comes in before Sunday we should all take it as a sign that we should go ahead.'

'How much had you in mind, Gina?' asked Timothy.

'Oh, it's not for me to say. I might be suspected of having inside knowledge of what was coming. And there's nothing I can give this week either. Perhaps someone from those opposing the move could suggest a figure.'

The idea was debated eagerly for some minutes and Cyril Kent finally proposed a figure of £15,000, which would leave exactly £100,000 to go. It was agreed that this figure was not too large to be impossible, but it was too much to be raised by a hasty campaign, and Gordon agreed not to spend the week making a special effort. It was to be left to God to decide. Whatever came out of the blue would make their decision plain.

The vote was carried unanimously and the meeting broke up with a sense of excitement.

'That was a shrewd move, Gina,' said Gordon, as they walked wearily up Highwood Avenue. 'You got us to vote unanimously, put the whole thing on a spiritual footing and bought us another week. The vote would certainly have gone against us otherwise.'

'I'm sure it would,' said Gina, 'but we have stuck our necks out, haven't we? £15,000 from nowhere in five days. It sounds like madness.'

'Let's call it faith,' said Gordon.

Shelley makes a move

If Gordon was exercising faith it certainly seemed to be rewarded swiftly. On the Tuesday morning there was hardly time to think about church affairs. It was Shelley's ninth birthday. Cards came tumbling through the letterbox, and Shelley, who had been in a fever of excitement since dawn, actually caught some of them before they reached the hall floor. She bore them off in triumph to open in her bedroom and, in her hurry, failed to notice a small brown envelope addressed to G. Barber Esq. which found its way into the waste-paper basket with the envelopes from the cards.

Shelley's party was that evening. Loud music greeted Gordon's ears as he reluctantly approached the house from the station to find that it had been occupied by hordes of shrieking teeny-boppers, playing noisy games and listening to, or rather shouting over, the latest release from Bloodfang and an unbelievable new album from Hovermower Factory which Shelley had received from a modernized aunt.

It was nearly midnight when Margaret and Gordon had restored the house to near-normality, and Margaret was taking Shelley's waste-paper basket to the refuse bin when she happened to notice the brown envelope. The letter it contained was from the district council, and it promised a grant of £10,000 towards the building fund 'for historic building maintenance'. Gordon had almost forgotten his application and had given it up for a lost cause.

Two thirds of the sum required all in one go! Gordon decided that it was worth getting Gina out of bed to tell her the news. But Gina was a heavy sleeper and did not hear the telephone, so the news had to wait until Wednesday.

On Wednesday evening Gordon arrived home to find Shelley looking very solemn and holding an envelope in her hand.

'This is for the church fund, Daddy,' she said, and gave him the envelope. There was £5 note in it.

'But Shelley, you can't afford this, surely?' said Gordon, astonished.

'Yes. I had it yesterday to buy records and I think I've got enough records for a bit. So I prayed about it and Jesus said I should give it to you.'

Shelley looked as if she were about to burst into tears and suddenly ran upstairs.

£10,005 and three days to go.

The crunch

But nothing arrived on the Thursday. A cheque for
£25 came in on the Friday but things were looking
grim. Eagerly Gordon looked for the post on Saturday
morning but there was nothing. By tea-time on Saturday Gordon 'phoned Timothy and told him that it
looked as if the cause was lost. By £4,970.

Gordon was about to get into bed when the front
doorbell rang. Margaret unbolted it and peered into
the darkness, with a hand on the safety chain. It was
Nigel.

'Sorry to bother you, Margaret. I was going to give
Gordon this tomorrow morning, but I was just passing
and I saw the light and somehow I thought I would give
it him now. See you tomorrow. 'Bye.'

The deep hum of the BMW rose and then fell again.
Gordon's trembling fingers almost prevented him from
opening the envelope. But there it was, a cheque for
£5,000. He looked at the clock. It was 11.45 p.m. This
time he held on until Gina did answer the phone.

- How do you decide how much to give to
  church/charities?
- How much of it ought to go overseas, to feed
  the hungry?
- Does God guide these decisions? How?

16

The Great Contest: Nigel

Nigel Rogers walked deliberately and slowly down the wide steps that led from the revolving doors of Crieff-Farbsteen to the pavement where ordinary mortals came and went.

Something jolted his memory, a memory of a reading from Genesis in the Bible, when Adam and Eve had been turned out of the Garden of Eden. Angelic beings had been set to guard the way back and a sword flashed to and fro. Now the commissionaire stood at the top of the steps with his hands behind his back. He did not say 'Good morning, sir' as Nigel left. He knew why Nigel was leaving the building at 9.30 a.m. The revolving doors flashed to and fro as the sunlight caught them. Nigel was no longer the rising star in the firmament of Crieff-Farbsteen. Nigel was no longer a member of their staff. He was sacked.

'Hogwood wants to see you'

The morning had started well. This short journey from the flat to the office was so much easier than the long haul from Canwell Park on the District Line. The sun was shining and he felt at ease with his conscience now he had handed his cheque over to Gordon. It seemed to have pleased Gordon for some reason too. He was going to hear about it one day.

Plans for the wedding were getting under way now and Sallie seemed to have accepted his staying at a distance. The preparation classes were over and they had been helpful. But the main reason for Nigel's cheerfulness was a deep, warm feeling at the back of his mind that there really was a new dimension to life beyond the material and self-centred demands of the City. These lunch-hour services were the thing he looked forward to twice a week. He couldn't believe all that he was hearing, nor could he call himself a Christian, but he found the talks and the readings from the Bible were making sense as an alternative view of life. Once you swallowed the incredible idea that God might be really *there*, the rest of it hung together. But although he was not convinced that God was really there he felt a wholesomeness about the people and the place. He would go again tomorrow.

Then came the brief message: 'Hogwood wants to see you.' Nothing unusual about that. Hogwood often wanted to see people. It was a fairly routine matter for a Monday morning. Nigel had grabbed the file he thought most likely to be needed and, whistling quietly, knocked on the heavy oaken door.

Two-and-a-half minutes later, a stunned Nigel Rogers had stumbled down the thickly carpeted corridor, carrying his file, which he would no longer need, and fingering his bunch of keys from which the car keys must soon be surrendered. His world had, in an instant, lurched sideways so that nothing seemed real any more. He had known that this might happen, but now, as he walked down those steps, it had happened. It was as if a switch had been thrown and the sunlight was a spotlight, seeking him out and shouting to the world, 'This was Nigel Rogers. He used to have a BMW. He's got to walk now. This *was* Nigel Rogers. . .'

The firm was being re-organized. Nigel's department would be merged with another. He was redundant as of the end of the month. But he would not be needed in the office.

He returned mechanically to the underground car-park, and fingered his few personal belongings from the BMW: the road atlas, the tin of mints, Sallie's gloves and an assortment of pens, pencils, tokens for cutlery which he did not want and a cassette or two which he no longer felt he wanted to hear. These he could keep. The car he could not keep.

Nigel wandered vaguely through the crowded streets and found himself sitting in the nave of St Paul's Cathedral.

It was natural to come here, he supposed. But was it? This great building with the cross on top of it was trying to tell the world that God was interested in it. If he was, thought Nigel, he didn't seem interested in Nigel. He realized for the first time, and with a sickening shock, that by the end of the month he would have lost not only his BMW, but his salary as well. How could Sallie go on paying the mortgage and run her car and feed them both? But they weren't married yet anyway. Sallie might not want him any more. The successful young businessman was an attractive proposition but an out-of-work ex-yuppie might not be quite her scene.

What kind of God was it that these Christians worshipped? You left your girlfriend so that you weren't living in sin; you gave up your spare time to church meetings and services; you even went to church in the middle of the week and got persecuted for it; and he laughed in your face and stood aside while your boss gave you three weeks' notice. Was this God's gratitude for a cheque for £5,000?

£5,000. . .he'd just given £5,000 to the church! What had he been thinking of? And God had pocketed the money without saying thanks. . .

No, that was ridiculous. He didn't believe in God so how could he be responsible for all this disaster? It came as a great surprise to Nigel to realize that he did blame God and that he therefore did believe that he existed. It was a strange way to come to believe and it wasn't in the least comfortable, nor did it seem to help him at all but Nigel believed in God.

And he wished that he didn't.

And he wished that he could have his £5,000 back.

St Wolfy's again

Tuesday lunch-time and the midday service. How near he had been to deciding not to come! How could he face his old colleagues again? How could he have anything to do with the City?

Yet strangely it had been Sallie who had persuaded him to go. Sallie had been wonderful when he broke the news. No recriminations, not even 'I told you so'. He had found in Sallie that first spark of comfort and encouragement that penetrates the dreadful gloom of a bereavement. And it was not just the warmth of her arms as she held him while he broke down and sobbed unashamedly. It was the realization that Sallie was someone who really loved him and who really supported him when he needed her. He had valued her for her stunning good looks and her ambitious view of life which had coincided with his own. He was glad of her salary, her connections in society and her cheerfulness, even if she did lose her temper sometimes. But now he had seen an unexpected and heart-warming compassion and strength of character in Sallie and it had given him new hope. If she could react like that, then they stood a good chance of surviving sickness and health together.

And Sallie had encouraged him to go to the service today. 'I think it will help,' was all that she would say. So here he was, behind his usual pillar, bewildered and battered and wondering still how God could be a God of love. He had spent a sleepless night, wrestling with the question, how could a God of love be so cruel? And he had no answer.

The strange thing was that the more he struggled with the question and the longer it remained unanswered, the more determined Nigel became. Something was going on here, but he could not reconcile two contradictory convictions. The first was that this

God-business made complete sense once you got over the hurdle of believing that there was a God. And he had. It all fitted together. God had made the world and given mankind freewill. Mankind had gone its own way. God had appeared in human form, in Jesus Christ, and had given himself up to ransom men and women. Nigel believed all that. But the second conviction rose from the pit of his stomach to meet the first.

This God of the Bible and doctrine and the church was playing cruel games with Nigel. How could you fall into the loving arms of a God who was beating you about the head and shoulders and then kicking you when you were down? Was it possible that the talk this lunch-time could help him with these questions?

'Where were you?'

The speaker announced his chosen subject – Job. The Old Testament again. Job of all people! The story of a man who had friends who came to him when he was down and told him what a sinner he was. Job's comforters. That was just what Nigel didn't need.

But the speaker was describing Job's plight, a man whose world had fallen about his ears. He had lost everything, his children, his house, his possessions, the lot. Only his wife remained. Nigel could identify with all of this. And when the reader read Job chapter three Nigel almost believed that it had been written precisely for him:

> *'Why did I not perish at birth, and die as I came from the womb?. . .For now I would*

141

be lying down in peace; I would be asleep and at rest. . .Why is life given to a man whose way is hidden, whom God has hedged in? . . .What I feared has come upon me; what I dreaded has happened to me. I have no peace, no quietness; I have no rest, but only turmoil' (Job 3:11, 13, 23, 25–26).

That was it exactly. God had hedged Job in and God had hedged Nigel in as well. How was the preacher going to get out of that one?

The preacher seemed in no hurry to bring a theological rabbit out of his hat. He described how the book of Job wound on, chapter after chapter, with Job getting increasingly frustrated but still hoping against hope that God would do something to rescue him.

Then, just when Job had reached the end of his tether, pleaded his innocence and longed for the days when God seemed real to him, and listened to interminable lectures from his 'friends', just when all was at the lowest possible ebb, God confronted Job with a question:

'Where were you when I laid the earth's foundation?'

Suddenly Job saw the point. The universe was not invented for his sake. The fact that he had suffered was terrible and God was not unmindful of his problem, but Job was not in a position to challenge God about all this. The whole sweep of nature swung before his mind's eye as he understood the grandeur of it all, and the Lord said to Job, 'Let him who accuses God answer him!'

And Job answered the Lord, 'I am unworthy – how can I reply to you? I put my hand over my mouth' (Job 40:1–2).

The speaker was not an evangelist and he made no call for his hearers to get up out of their seats, but no more powerful appeal could have been made to Nigel. That was it. The missing ingredient: I am unworthy. If God really was God, then the right thing to do was to bow to him, not argue with him. The fact that the book of Job finished with Job twice as prosperous as he ever had been and living to a contented 140 years old was neither here nor there. Nigel knelt with the rest for the prayer at the end of the service. He had not solved the problem of God's apparent carelessness for Nigel's feelings and circumstances, but he had allowed God to solve a much deeper problem, the separation between them both.

In two days Nigel had lost his job and his self-esteem and found his God and hope. What a bargain!

- Does God reward his people with unfailing health and wealth? If not, can you explain his attitude?
- What matters most, God's protection of me or his glory in the universe?
- Where were you when he laid the earth's foundation?

17

Whatever happened to Jacob?

Sallie expected Nigel to be in the house before her that afternoon, so when she turned her car into the driveway and saw the BMW she was not surprised. Then she remembered. Nigel would soon have no BMW. But he seemed quite uncharacteristically excited about something. Perhaps the shock of losing his job had made him delirious.

'I followed your advice, Sallie,' he began, as soon as they had embraced.

'That's a change,' said Sallie. 'What will you drink?'

'Coffee, please.'

That was a change too, thought Sallie. He usually reached for something rather stronger.

'No, it's important. I followed your advice and went

to St Wolfy's again. And it's made all the difference. I've seen the point of it all. I suppose you would have to say that I've become a Christian.'

There was a stunned silence.

'You mean got *converted*?'

'Oh no, nothing like that. I mean I've seen the point of it all. This guy today said, "Let Jesus in." So I did!'

'And that's not being converted?'

'I don't know what the technical terms are but it makes sense of life.'

'Look, Nigel, sit down quietly and drink your coffee while I have my shower and then you can tell me quite rationally what's been going on.'

Holy Joe

So Nigel did as he was told and waited impatiently for Sallie to finish her home-coming rituals. He couldn't help feeling that she was taking a long time over it on purpose. At last, however, she reappeared, sat opposite him in her usual chair and prepared to give him her full attention.

'Begin at the beginning,' said Sallie. 'You went to St Wolfy's to get a bit of encouragement.'

'I don't know why I went. I was on automatic. Mainly because you suggested it. Anyway, I got a lot more than encouragement. This chap, Paul somebody or other, was talking about Job.'

'*Job*?'

'Yes, you know, the Old Testament character who got clobbered because he was so saintly and Old Nick wanted to prove that he would curse God and die.'

'So you're the one who felt clobbered.'

'Quite so. Why should I suffer so much when I was innocent? I lost my job because I was honest. I nearly lost you because my conscience wouldn't let me stay here. Every time I do something right I get punished for it!'

'Holy Joe,' muttered Sallie.

'That's exactly it!' said Nigel excitedly. 'God said to Job, "Where were you when I created the universe?" or words to that effect. "You think you're so innocent but you're keeping me at arm's length by your self-righteousness. You are unworthy." That was the word that hit me. I was unworthy. However good you are, you are unworthy where God is concerned. It wasn't encouragement I needed. It was forgiveness. These people at St Barnabas' are right after all. It's in the Bible. We all need forgiving.'

Sallie cut him off.

'Nigel! You're preaching!'

'Sorry,' said Nigel, and he really meant it.

'Let me quote your exact words when we went to see Timothy and Diana,' said Sallie. 'I was so impressed that I wrote them down. "You are expecting us to be a morbid, medieval pack of grovelling, sin-sodden morons." That's what you said, and now you're becoming one too, I suppose.'

Nigel ignored her remark.

'Do you remember what Timothy said next, though? I didn't write it down but it was something like, "The whole point of Christianity is forgiveness." You can't come to God by being good and hoping for a good report. The thing is that we are all "living in sin". Diana said that, didn't she? I thought it was a joke. But I see now what she meant. When we recognize that we're in the wrong God comes in and puts us right.'

Sallie's mind was working quickly as usual.

146

'I'm glad you've found something positive just when you were in need of it. No. I know you'll accuse me of saying that you've "got religion" as a substitute for a good job. But there is a question here, isn't there? Will "coming to Christ", or whatever you call it, get you another job, or are you so heavenly-minded now that you see no earthly use in having a job? You know, "God will provide", and all that?'

'I've been thinking about that, too,' said Nigel, pulling a Bible out of his pocket. 'I've had all afternoon to think about it. And I've been reading more of the book of Job.'

'What *is* all this Job? Why is he so important all of a sudden?'

'It's the book before Psalms. Nobody knows who wrote it or when but some people think it was a very ancient story, one of the oldest in the Bible. See – I've done my homework! But when I got to chapter 28 it just seemed to answer those very questions.'

'Man's hand assaults the flinty rock'

'It's a wonderful description of mankind's search for wisdom. And it gives a vivid picture of mining – how far people will go to dig wealth out of the ground. Listen:

> *'Man puts an end to the darkness;*
> *he searches the farthest recesses*
> *for ore in the blackest darkness.*
> *Far from where people dwell he cuts a*
> *shaft,*
> *in places forgotten by the foot of man;*
> *far from men he dangles and sways. . .*

Man's hand assaults the flinty rock
and lays bare the roots of the mountains
(Job 28:3–9).

'And so on. All that for material gain, digging jewels out of the earth.

'Then he says, "But where can wisdom be found?" Not in mining for metal. What's the point? Not in the sea. Not in death. Not in life at all. The point is that we can't discover it unaided. We don't understand the *reason* for it all. But in verse 23 it says, "God understands the way to it and he alone knows where it dwells."

'Are you with me? All this having a good job and getting on in the world is like digging in a hole to find buried treasure and you never find it. Only God can reveal what life is for, so we have to stop digging and ask him to tell us.'

'And what does he tell us?' asked Sallie, 'and does the job have a pension? Someone said that a few months ago in my hearing.'

'He tells us,' said Nigel, again ignoring the second question, 'that "The fear of the Lord – that is wisdom, and to shun evil is understanding." I think that's very clear confirmation that I was wrong to be where I was with Crieff-Farbsteen. "Shun evil". That bonds issue was evil, potentially.'

'But you didn't resign. You were pushed.'

'Exactly. I didn't see it clearly at all. I was too busy digging for jewels in the mine to hear what God was trying to say. I think I might even be grateful to Hogwood one of these days. I can't feel it yet, but the shock may have done me good after all. And the fear of the Lord (that means "awe" or seeing that God is real), that came afterwards. But it *is* real, and Sallie darling, it's the most wonderful realization I've ever discovered.

'As to getting another job, I don't see why we shouldn't give God a trial there too. Maybe he's got something lined up for us!'

Sallie looked at Nigel with a mixture of bewilderment, love and admiration.

'The Reverend Nigel Rogers, DD, perhaps? Nigel, I think you're insane! I expect it's the shock of losing your job that's made you like this. I don't know what's got into you, but. . .'

'But what?'

'But I hope it stays there.'

'We've been very sane together for a year or two,' said Nigel, 'why not be insane together now?'

'I don't understand this at all,' said Sallie, 'but I do love you. So much that I might even be a vicar's wife one day.'

'Sallie, you don't mean that, do you?'

'No,' said Sallie, 'I don't.'

Somehow Nigel's half-consumed cup of coffee got knocked over but neither of them noticed.

When you've met God, what happens next?

The author of the book of Genesis seems to lose interest in Jacob after the career climax wrestling event at Peniel. He seems anxious to move on to the story of Joseph, in which Jacob, now Israel, plays the part of the bereaved Patriarch, mourning the loss of his wife and then his children and finishing his life as an Egyptian mummy.

Really?

Yes, look at Genesis 50:1–3.

But before all that, Genesis 35 sketches in the outline of the rest of Jacob's life in Canaan. It is clear that he is a genuinely changed man. He is responsive to God's call ('go up to Bethel and settle there', verse 1). He purges the idols from his household ('"Get rid of the foreign gods you have with you". . .Jacob buried them under the oak at Shechem', verses 2, 4).

God appeared to Jacob again, confirming his new name Israel and renewing his promise of the possession of the land for his descendants (verses 11–12). God's blessing did not shield Israel from sorrow, however. The unpalatable truth is recorded and not glossed over. Rachel, his beloved, died giving birth to Benjamin and was buried 'on the way to Bethlehem'. As if that was not enough, Reuben, the eldest son, incestuously slept with Bilhah, who could reasonably be described as his own aunt. 'Israel heard of it', we are told. What he said or did about it we do not know.

Finally he returned to Mamre near Hebron and was present at the death of his father Isaac, 'old and full of years. And his sons Esau and Jacob buried him.'

What is to be said about Jacob, a man who lived about 4,000 years ago? How long is his inheritance? How many generations of self-centred people have used other people and tried to use God to attain their material ends, only to discover that God was really pursuing them, relentlessly but quietly, with the gentle weapon of wisdom in his hand?

Is it true that a selfish, materialistic, spoilt mother's darling, known by his very name as a swindler and cheat, could meet God, submit to him and be radically changed so that he could find his place in the hall of the heroes of faith? The author of the letter to the Hebrews thought so:

> *By faith Jacob, when he was dying, blessed each of Joseph's sons, and worshipped as he leaned on the top of his staff* (Hebrews 11:21).

What was his secret? Did he try to reform himself? make good resolutions? join a society? No, he came to a point in life when the going was too heavy for him and he looked up and. . .there was God. That was not all. He reached out and clung to God and from that point on, God remained with him.

Francis Thomson's *The Hound of Heaven* might well have been written as a commentary on Jacob's career:

> *I fled Him down the nights and down the days;*
> *I fled Him down the arches of the years;*
> *I fled Him down the labyrinthine ways*
> *of my own mind; and in the midst of tears*
> *I hid from Him, and under running laughter. . .*
> > *Halts by me that footfall:*
> > *Is my gloom, after all.*
> *Shade of his hand, outstretched caressingly?*
> > *'Ah, fondest, blindest, weakest,*
> > *I am He whom thou seekest!*
> *Thou dravest love from thee, who dravest Me.'*

- If you find God as a result of a crisis in your life, does that mean that the meeting is not real?
- If you lost a leg and God offered you a crutch, would you accept it?

18

Knots tied

Sallie Rogers (née Peterson), resplendent in her wedding gown, laughed with everyone else. Nigel had just begun his speech with the required formula, 'My wife and I' and had elicited the usual round of applause.

The 'Candelabra Room' in the Mansion Hotel, Canford Heath, was full of guests from Derbyshire, Suffolk, the City and Canwell Park. The Hon. Mrs Peterson, Sallie's mother, had been unable to understand why so many 'locals', as she put it, had to be invited, but she had acquiesced and was sitting now at the top table beneath a huge yellow hat, delicately sipping her champagne whenever a toast was proposed.

Lieutenant-Colonel Fitzpaine Rogers cut a gallant figure as he had insisted on wearing his full dress uniform including a sword. Nigel had protested vigorously that he looked like the very model of a modern major general, but his father was not to be moved from his decision.

The only jarring note had been the last-minute refusal of Sallie's father to come south of the Border to give away the bride. His twenty-two-year estrangement from the rest of his family was too great a chasm to cross, so a willing uncle had been imported from Huntingdon to do the job. His speech had been full of racy, indeed risqué, anecdotes from Sallie's youth, but on such happy days these things are forgiven.

Now Nigel was on his feet saying complimentary and not entirely true things about Shelley Barber and Emma Peterson, the two bridesmaids, and telling the tired joke about his buying a book called 'How to hug' in a second-hand bookshop, only to find that it was part ten of an encyclopedia. A glazed expression stole over the faces of the guests and they began to eye their champagne hopefully. But Nigel had something else to say.

How could decent people do such a thing?

'There are two important things, I should say two *other* important things, I want to tell you. Some of you know about them but most of you do not. One is good news, the other is both good and bad.'

There was interest now. This was different. Some news was about to be announced. Perhaps it wasn't going to be merely stale jokes after all. Good news. Now what would that be? The Lieutenant-Colonel whispered to his wife, with approval, that there was obviously a child on the way. Good and bad, what could that be? Good, that Nigel had had a big promotion with Crieff-Farbsteen; bad, that it meant they had to go and live in Australia. All these thoughts ricocheted through the minds of the guests while Nigel paused to draw breath.

'The good – bad news is that I'm out of work.'

The expectant hum ceased abruptly. The only movement discernible was the Lieutenant-Colonel's monocle falling from his incredulous eye. Even if it was true, and not all the family had been told, what a time to mention it now! How could members of the Rogers clan hold up their heads when the bridegroom, the man of the day, was on the scrap-heap? And Nigel seemed to be passing it off as partly good news! What kind of bravado was this?

'It's bad because nobody likes being out of work. But it's good because I've realized, we've realized' (he looked fondly at Sallie) 'that my job was too pressurized, too materialistic and too selfish. All I was doing was destroying other people so that I could get to the top.'

This was too much for his father.

'It's either them or you in this world,' he said more loudly than a stage whisper. His wife put a restraining hand on his arm.

Nigel paused and then went on.

'The second bit of news Sallie and I owe to our parents. We haven't told them this yet, but we have both decided to join St Barnabas' Church, Canwell Park. I have given my life to Jesus Christ.'

The shock produced by the first announcement was as nothing compared to this. Sallie's mother gave a little scream and knocked her champagne over. She wondered whether to faint but decided that she should keep that weapon in reserve, in case of even worse revelations to come.

Joining a church was bad enough, but 'giving your life to Jesus Christ' sounded like. . .like Billy Graham, or revivalism or something. How could *decent* people do such a thing and admit it in public as if it was an advantage of some kind?

And then to say that they owed it to their *parents*! But Nigel was speaking again.

'You notice that I said that *I* have taken this step. Sallie is totally with me in this but she thought it would be jumping the gun to say that she has taken it, yet.'

'She will do soon, dear.'

Connie Bassett's voice could not be compared to a stage whisper by any stretch of the imagination. Some guests laughed, others were even further embarrassed. How had *that* woman got in here? 'She looks like a Pearly Queen,' thought Sallie's mother. She was wearing a quite ridiculous large yellow hat.

'And we owe all this, indirectly anyway, to our parents because it was they who persuaded us, against our will I might add, to get married at all and to get married in church. And we owe it to Timothy and Diana and all of you good people at St Barnabas' for welcoming us and giving us loving and patient instruction.

'Now it's Timothy's job to preach sermons and I won't try to preach one now. . .'

'Good!' The voice of an uncle in the corner produced a titter among some aunts.

'But I do want to explain that I'm not becoming a Christian for what I can get out of it. I am quite certain that grab-what-you-can-get is no way to enjoy life and that God loved the world and wants us all to love each other.'

For the majority of the guests this was dreadful. They looked at their empty plates and moved uncomfortably in their chairs. Even Timothy Monteith prayed silently that Nigel would know where to stop. This prayer was answered immediately, for Nigel went on to a few more aspects of gratitude to his parents, which they were able to accept and be quite pleased about. He sat down at last to a polite but less than rapturous ovation.

But the cake was magnificent and the wine had flowed. It had been 'a lovely service'. 'Weren't the flowers nice?' and 'Didn't Sallie look radiant?' Everything except Nigel's speech had been exactly as one might expect of a wedding. The Lieutenant-Colonel had a few sharp words with Nigel, the Hon. Mrs Peterson said nothing at all to Nigel and most people forgot about what he'd said. But the people of St Barnabas' were hugely encouraged by his public statement and Nigel was pleased that he'd decided to go ahead with it.

Now the period of uncertainty was over. They were back together, properly this time. As they were driven to the airport Sallie said,

'Do you remember how we very nearly didn't call at the Vicarage that first night?'

'I do, and you said, "We jolly well must." It was the best thing you could ever have said.'

Tainted source

'What I don't understand', said Diana Monteith, as she lowered herself thankfully into her armchair that evening, 'is why Nigel gave the church that enormous cheque. Well, God prompted him, I suppose, but what did Nigel mean by it?'

Timothy thought for a few moments.

'I think he was spontaneously responding to a growing conviction that God is real, and he responded in cash because that was what he was used to and he responded generously because he's a generous chap.'

'It came fifteen minutes before the deadline. Even old Cyril was convinced that God was behind that.'

'Yes,' said Timothy, 'but, you know, Gordon had had doubts whether we should accept the money. Because it came from a "tainted source".'

'Well, Gordon was glad enough to accept it as a sign of God's guidance, wasn't he? That's a bit pharisaical.'

'Yes, but Sallie persuaded him that if you question the route by which money comes to the church you'd never have any money at all.'

'Clever girl.'

'But there is another problem, you know.'

'Which is?'

'Ought we to give it back? Now he's lost his job, Nigel needs the money more than the church does.'

'If we gave it him back,' said Diana slowly, 'would we be admitting that God hadn't answered our prayer?

People would accuse us of borrowing the £5,000 just to meet the demands of the agreement.'

'It might be a problem, I agree,' said Timothy, 'but I've put it to Nigel and he's quite adamant that he doesn't want the money back. He says it would be immoral. I'm amazed at how far he's come in such a short time.'

'Well, he's always been a very upright young man with a well-developed conscience, hasn't he? I wonder whether he'll get another job?'

'He thinks he will. He's very optimistic.'

'They might have to sell the house.'

'If the Hon. Mrs doesn't bail them out I think they might, and Nigel's speech has probably sunk that source of support.'

'Well, I think those two deserve a break. While they were atheists they taught us a thing or two. And now – who knows what can happen?'

'Who knows indeed?' said Timothy, in the tone of voice that conveyed, 'I think we've talked enough and it's time for bed. It's Sunday tomorrow.'

Diana heard the unspoken message.

What makes young Rogers tick?

'What I don't understand', said Bob Renshaw as he and Gina Holwell walked slowly through Canwell Park on the way back to Fairview Avenue after the wedding, 'is what makes young Rogers tick. He's a clever chap but he does the weirdest things. He was very sure that he and Sallie were right to live together and he was quite certain that he was in the right job. The next thing we hear is that he's left her and then when he loses his job he tells everyone it was a rotten job anyway. And why didn't he tell Sallie what he meant to do instead of walking out and leaving a note?

'And what about Sallie? She was so upset that I didn't think she'd ever speak to him again. And now they're all lovey-dovey again. I think they're unstable, those two. I don't think that marriage will last.'

'I don't know about that,' said Gina thoughtfully. 'But I think Nigel's behaviour is easy to explain. He has a well-developed conscience for one thing. As soon as he understood that the church didn't like them living together he couldn't get it out of his mind. On the surface he argued and tried to convince himself and others that he and Sallie were right, but the louder his argument the more his conscience told him that his case was weak.

'The same with the job, you see. Once it was pointed out to him he couldn't escape from the nagging feeling that he was in the wrong place. I'm not sure why he left a note for Sallie like that. It was rather hurtful. He probably didn't consider what effect it would have on her. It seemed rather dramatic, I suppose, and it saved him having to face a row with her.'

'They had a row anyway.'

'Yes, he couldn't escape that.'

'And you said that what pulled Sallie out of despair was talking about her wedding dress. That doesn't sound like the whole story.'

'No,' admitted Gina, 'it probably wasn't, but I thought that if I could get her to focus on something real and practical she would stop going round in circles of despair. And any woman can be tempted to be interested in her own wedding dress. Especially someone like Sallie who looks a million pounds in anything she wears, and knows it too. I think that was the trigger that started her off on the positive track.'

They walked in silence for a while.

'Thinking of wedding dresses, Gina, we still haven't sorted US out.'

'I'm too old for a wedding dress,' said Gina firmly.

'But you're not too old for a wedding.'

There was another long silence.

'Was that meant to be a proposal?' asked Gina.

'Not really,' said Bob. 'But since it came out like one, let's say it was.'

'Despite all the problems we would have?'

'Yes.'

Another silence.

'Give me a week and I'll be definite.'

'Thanks,' said Bob, 'I'll be off now, then. Goodnight, Gina, love.'

'Goodnight, Bob,' said Gina.

- ■ If business and God's love collide, how can you reconcile them?
- ■ Is conscience really a better guide than expediency?
- ■ What authority have you got for your answer?
